CHRISTMAS SECRETS AT ASHFORD MANOR

Victorian Romance

FAYE GODWIN

Tica House Publishing

Sweet Romance that Delights and Enchant!

PERSONAL WORD FROM THE AUTHOR

DEAREST READERS,

I'm so delighted that you have chosen one of my books to read. I am proud to be a part of the team of writers at Tica House Publishing. Our goal is to inspire, entertain, and give you many hours of reading pleasure. Your kind words and loving readership are deeply appreciated.

I would like to personally invite you to sign up for updates and to become part of our **Exclusive Reader Club**—it's completely Free to Join! I'd love to welcome you!

Much love,

Faye Godwin

CONTENTS

PART I

CHAPTER 1

THE COTTAGE SMELLED of mutton stew and wood smoke, a comforting blend that had welcomed Samuel Hartwell home from the smithy every evening for as long as Opal could remember. She stirred the pot hanging over the fire, tasting the broth with the wooden spoon worn smooth by her mother's hands three years past. Not quite ready—the meat needed another quarter hour to become tender enough for her father.

Opal wiped her hands on her apron and moved to the small window, pressing her nose against the cool glass. Darkness had settled over the village like a heavy blanket, broken only by the occasional flicker of candlelight from neighbouring cottages. The smithy would be closed by now, Master Griggs having banked the forge fire hours ago, yet her father had not returned.

She pulled her mother's old shawl tighter around her shoulders and returned to her mending basket. Samuel's work shirt bore a fresh tear near the shoulder—the third this month. The coarse fabric was wearing thin from years of sparks and hard labour, but replacing it was beyond their means. Opal threaded her needle with careful precision, her small fingers nimble from years of practice. At twelve, she had been keeping house for three years, ever since consumption had claimed her mother and left father and daughter to fend for themselves.

The clock on the mantelpiece—a wedding gift from her mother's family—chimed nine times. Opal's stomach tightened with worry. Samuel was never this late without sending word. Perhaps Master Griggs had kept him to finish an urgent commission, or maybe they were discussing the new apprentice everyone said the smithy needed.

A sound outside made her look up from her stitching. Footsteps, but not her father's familiar measured tread. These were running feet, stumbling and desperate. Opal set aside her sewing and moved to the window again, but the lane remained shrouded in darkness.

The footsteps stopped at their cottage.

The door burst open with such violence that it slammed against the wall, rattling the dishes on the dresser. Samuel stood in the doorway, his face pale as chalk, blood trickling from a cut above his left eye. His usually neat hair was dishevelled, his shirt torn at the collar, and his hands shook as he gripped the doorframe.

"Papa!" Opal rushed to him, but he held up a warning hand.

"Listen to me carefully, child," he said, his voice low and urgent. He closed the door behind him and moved swiftly to the window, peering through the curtains into the darkness. "I've seen something terrible tonight. Murder, Opal. And the man who did it has the power to see me blamed for it."

"Murder?" The word fell from her lips like a stone into still water.

"Lord Ashford, h-he killed a man—a travelling merchant—for his purse of gold. I-I saw it happen near the old mill." Samuel's hands shook as he spoke. "But he spotted me there, Opal. He knows I witnessed it, and he's already moving to silence me. I heard him talking to Constable Morrison, spinning lies about me stealing from the smithy to cover his own crime."

Opal felt the world tilt beneath her feet. "But Papa, if you tell them what you saw—"

"Who would believe a blacksmith's assistant over Lord Ashford?" Samuel's laugh was bitter. "He owns half this village, including the magistrate who would hear any case. No, child. He'll frame me for theft, and I'll hang for it while he goes free."

The sound of distant voices made Samuel freeze. He moved to the window again, his face growing paler.

"They're searching the village already," he whispered. "I thought I had more time." He turned to face Opal, his expression anguished. "I want to take you with me, child. God knows I can't bear to leave you. But if we run together, they'll catch us both. You'd slow me down, and—" His voice cracked. "They'll punish a child as accomplice to a thief."

"Papa, no!" Opal grabbed his arm, terror making her voice shrill.

Samuel pulled something small and cold from his pocket, pressing it into her palm. "Hide this, child. Keep it safe always. One day it may be the only thing that proves your father was no thief."

Opal looked down at the object in her hand. It was a key, but unlike any she had seen before. Made of iron, it was small and intricately worked, with an unusual pattern of notches along its length. The metal was warm from her father's touch, and something about its weight suggested it was important beyond its simple appearance.

"Papa, I don't understand—"

"You will, in time. I-I've been hiding things. And I'll find more to hide." Samuel cupped her face in his work-roughened hands, his eyes bright with unshed tears. "Be strong, my brave girl. Remember that your father loved you more than life itself, and that everything I've taught you about right and wrong still holds true, no matter what lies they tell about me."

The sound of horses' hooves echoed from the lane, accompanied by the jingle of harness and the murmur of voices. Samuel's face went white.

"They're here." He kissed Opal's forehead quickly, then moved to the window and peered through a gap in the curtains. "Constable Morrison, and others. Too many others." He turned back to Opal, his expression desperate. "I must go. *Now*."

"Take me with you!" Opal grabbed his arm, terror making her voice shrill. "Please, Papa, don't leave me alone!"

"I can't, child. You'd slow me down, and besides—" His voice broke. "They might not hurt a child, but they'll surely kill me if they catch me. At least this way, you have a chance."

The voices outside grew louder, more urgent. Samuel pulled his old coat from its peg and shrugged it on, then hefted his bag onto his shoulder. At the door, he paused and looked back at Opal, who stood frozen in the centre of the room, still clutching the mysterious key.

"Remember what I've told you," he said softly. "Trust no one, especially not the Ashfords. And Opal—" He seemed to struggle with his words. "Whatever happens, whatever they say about me, know that I never stole so much as a bent nail. Your father is many things, but he's no thief."

Then he was gone, slipping out into the night like a shadow. Opal ran to the window and pressed her face against the glass, but the darkness had already swallowed him whole. She could hear the search party moving through the village, their voices calling Samuel's name, their torches casting dancing shadows on the cottage walls.

Opal sank onto her mother's old chair beside the fire, the iron key clutched so tightly in her fist that its edges bit into her palm. The mutton stew bubbled cheerfully in its pot, filling the cottage with the aroma of home and safety—things that seemed as distant now as her mother's gentle laughter.

Outside, the voices spread out as the search broadened. But Opal knew they would return. Did these men not know where her father lived? Why hadn't they come here first? Whatever her father had witnessed, whatever crime he had stumbled upon, the consequences were already thundering toward their little cottage like a runaway horse. She could only wait, and pray, and try to be as brave as her father believed her to be.

The clock chimed ten, then eleven. Still Opal sat by the dying fire, watching the shadows dance on the walls and listening for footsteps that might herald either her father's return or the arrival of those who sought to destroy him. The key in her hand grew warm with her body heat, a small anchor of hope in a world suddenly turned upside down.

When dawn finally crept across the windowsill, painting the cottage walls with pale gold light, Opal realised with a sick certainty that her father would not be coming home. But the men hadn't come? Had they caught him? Was his fate already sealed? Whatever new life awaited her would begin with the sunrise, and she could only pray that Samuel's trust in her strength would prove justified.

The sound of horses' hooves returned with the dawn light.

This time, they stopped at her gate and did not move on.

Opal rose from her chair on unsteady legs, the key still clutched in her hand, she went to face whatever judgement the morning would bring. Through the window, she could see the constable dismounting from his horse, his face grim beneath his dark cap. Behind him rode two other men—one she recognised as Master Griggs from the smithy, his expression troubled and sad.

The third rider made her stomach clench with fear. Even at twelve, Opal knew the cut of fine clothes and the bearing of authority. Lord Ashford sat his black gelding like a king surveying his domain, his pale eyes fixed on their cottage with an expression of cold satisfaction. Beside him, on a smaller horse, rode a boy near her own age with dark hair and fine features—Master Edmund, the lord's younger son.

As the men approached her door, Opal quickly slipped the key down the front of her dress, feeling its cool weight settle against her heart, then slip to her waist. Whatever was about to happen, whatever accusations were about to be made, she would keep her father's trust. The key would remain hidden, waiting for the day when it might serve the purpose he had intended.

The knock on the door, when it came, was neither gentle nor patient.

CHAPTER 2

THE GREY LIGHT of dawn revealed the full scope of Opal's catastrophe. She stood frozen at her cottage window, now clutching her mother's worn Bible, watching as Constable Morrison methodically searched their modest home under Lord Ashford's cold and intrusive supervision.

"Turn over every stone, Morrison," Lord Ashford commanded from his position near the fireplace, his pale eyes surveying the simple furnishings with obvious distaste. "A thief who would steal from his own employer surely keeps his ill-gotten gains close at hand."

Master Griggs stood near the door, his weathered face creased with obvious discomfort. "My lord, Samuel Hartwell has worked for me these eight years past. Never once have I known him to take so much as a nail that wasn't his due."

"Then you've been deceived by a master criminal," Lord Ashford replied smoothly. "The evidence will speak for itself."

Opal pressed herself against the wall as Constable Morrison approached her parents' bedroom, his heavy boots echoing on the wooden floor. Lord Ashford had already been inside the room, though he hadn't discovered anything. But she knew they would find nothing—her father was the most honest man in the village, careful to account for every tool, every scrap of metal that passed through his hands. Whatever Lord Ashford claimed Samuel had stolen was surely a fabrication designed to explain away the nobleman's own crimes.

"Here!" Morrison's voice carried a note of surprise from the bedroom. "My lord, you'd best see this."

Lord Ashford strode past Opal without a glance, his fine clothes rustling with authority. From the bedroom came the sound of furniture being moved, then Morrison's voice again, heavy with satisfaction.

"Found it beneath the mattress, my lord. A leather pouch, and it's heavy with coin."

Opal's blood turned to ice. Impossible. Her father kept their meagre savings in a tin box on the kitchen shelf—perhaps two shillings and sixpence in total, earned through years of careful economy. There was no leather pouch, no heavy purse of coins.

"Let me see." Lord Ashford's voice carried the tone of a man whose expectations had been perfectly met. "Ah yes, gold coins. Foreign, by the look of them. Exactly what one might expect from selling stolen iron tools to merchants bound for distant parts."

They emerged from the bedroom, Morrison carrying a brown leather pouch that Opal had never seen before in her life. Lord Ashford's pale eyes glittered with triumph as he examined the contents, spilling several gold coins into his palm where they caught the morning light.

"But my lord," Master Griggs protested, "I've not reported any tools missing from my smithy. How can you be certain—"

"Because I took inventory myself last evening, after Hartwell failed to return from his duties," Lord Ashford cut him off smoothly. "Two hammers, a set of tongs, and three iron bars— all missing. No doubt sold to fund whatever vice has corrupted an otherwise honest man."

Opal wanted to scream that it was all lies, that her father would never steal anything, that the pouch must have been planted there. But the words stuck in her throat as Lord Ashford's cold gaze finally settled on her. There was something in those pale eyes that made her skin crawl—a calculating look that seemed to weigh her value like a merchant appraising goods.

"Which brings us to the matter of the child," Lord Ashford

said, his voice deceptively gentle. "Orphaned now, with nowhere to go and no family to claim her."

"Maybe she has family," Master Griggs said quickly. "I could find out—"

"Nonsense. The child is my responsibility now, as landlord of this cottage and employer of her criminal father." Lord Ashford moved closer to Opal, close enough that she could smell the expensive soap he used and see the cold calculation in his eyes. "Besides, it would be unchristian to cast out a child, regardless of her father's sins."

Morrison nodded approvingly. "Very generous of you, my lord."

"Indeed. I shall take her into service at the manor. Honest work will help her overcome the unfortunate example set by her father." Lord Ashford's smile was thin and sharp as a blade. "She can start in the scullery—good hard labour to teach her the value of what her father so carelessly threw away."

Young Master Edmund, who had remained silent throughout the search, finally spoke from his position near the door. "Father, surely she could serve as a housemaid instead? She's only a child—"

"Precisely why she must learn discipline," Lord Ashford cut his son off with icy authority. "The scullery will suit her perfectly. Mrs. Grimwald can see to her training."

Opal's heart sank at the mention of Mrs. Grimwald, Ashford Manor's feared head housekeeper. Every servant in the village knew of the woman's harsh temperament and quick hand with a birch rod. To serve under her would be little better than prison.

"My lord," she said, finding her voice at last, "might I gather a few of my mother's things? Her prayer book, perhaps, and—"

"You may take the clothes on your back and nothing more," Lord Ashford replied curtly. "Everything else in this cottage belongs to the estate, as recompense for your father's theft. Even the furnishings will be sold to help recover our losses."

Master Griggs looked as though he wanted to protest, but Lord Ashford's warning glance silenced him. Opal clutched her mother's Bible tighter, grateful she had thought to hide it beneath her shawl. The key her father had given her pressed cold against her skin, hidden beneath her bodice where no searching eyes could find it.

"Come along then, child," Lord Ashford commanded. "Mrs. Grimwald will be expecting you, and she dislikes tardiness above all other faults."

As they prepared to leave, Opal cast one last desperate look around the cottage that had been her world. The mutton stew still sat in its pot over the cold ashes of last night's fire, a mocking reminder of the normal evening she had expected. Her sewing basket remained beside her mother's chair,

Samuel's torn shirt waiting for mending that would never come.

"Move along," Morrison said, not unkindly but with obvious impatience. "The magistrate will want my report on this business."

They walked through the village in a grim procession—Lord Ashford mounted on his black gelding, young Master Edmund on his smaller bay, while Opal trudged behind on foot with Constable Morrison's heavy hand on her shoulder. Neighbours peered from their windows and doorways, their faces mixing curiosity with pity. Some whispered among themselves, no doubt already spreading the tale of Samuel Hartwell's fall from grace.

Ashford Manor loomed ahead like a great stone beast crouched on the hillside, its mullioned windows reflecting the grey morning sky. Opal had passed it countless times but never imagined she would enter its gates as anything other than a visitor delivering eggs or vegetables from their small garden. Now those gates seemed to yawn like a mouth ready to swallow her whole.

The manor's courtyard bustled with morning activity—stable boys leading horses to water, kitchen maids hurrying with baskets of bread, gardeners wheeling barrows of autumn vegetables toward the kitchen garden. All of them stopped their work to stare as Lord Ashford rode through with his unlikely prisoner.

Mrs. Grimwald stood waiting at the servants' entrance, her tall, angular frame clothed in severe black bombazine. Her steel-grey hair was pulled back so tightly it seemed to stretch the skin around her pale eyes, and her thin mouth was set in a permanent expression of disapproval. She looked Opal up and down as though examining a questionable piece of meat.

"So, it's true then. And this is the thief's daughter," she said, her voice carrying the crisp authority of long command. "Small for her age, and soft-looking. Kitchen work will remedy that soon enough."

"See that it does," Lord Ashford replied, dismounting from his horse. "The child needs to learn the value of honest labour, having been raised by a criminal father. Start her in the scullery and work her up from there—if she proves worthy."

Mrs. Grimwald's smile was as warm as winter wind. "Of course, my lord. She'll earn every scrap of food and every hour of sleep, I assure you."

As Lord Ashford strode away toward the manor's main entrance, young Master Edmund lingered for a moment, his dark eyes meeting Opal's with what might have been sympathy. But a sharp word from his father sent him hurrying after, leaving Opal alone with Mrs. Grimwald's calculating stare.

"Come along then," the housekeeper commanded, turning on her heel and marching toward the servants' entrance. "Time to see what manner of work awaits the daughter of a thief."

The servants' entrance led into a stone-flagged corridor that smelled of lye soap and boiled cabbage. Mrs. Grimwald's boots clicked like a death march on the worn stones as she led Opal deeper into the manor's working heart. They passed the still room, where Opal glimpsed shelves lined with preserves and pickled vegetables, then the butler's pantry with its gleaming silver and crystal.

Finally, they reached the scullery—a low-ceilinged room dominated by a huge stone sink and wooden drying racks that stretched from floor to ceiling. The air was thick with steam from great copper pots bubbling over the fire, and the floor was slick with spilled water and kitchen scraps.

"This will be your domain," Mrs. Grimwald announced with obvious satisfaction. "Every pot, every pan, every dish that passes through this kitchen will come to you for cleaning. You'll scrub until your hands bleed, and then you'll scrub some more."

A girl of perhaps sixteen looked up from where she knelt scrubbing a large copper pot, her face red from the heat and her arms wet to the elbows. She gave Opal a look of mingled pity and relief—pity for what Opal faced, and likely relief that she was no longer the lowest in the servants' hierarchy.

"This is Jenny," Mrs. Grimwald continued. "She'll show you what's expected, though I doubt you'll prove as capable as she. Jenny came to us from honest folk, not thieves and murderers."

The words hit Opal like physical blows, but she forced herself to stand straight and meet Mrs. Grimwald's cold stare. Whatever lay ahead, she would endure it. Her father had trusted her to be strong, and she would not disappoint him.

"You'll sleep in the servants' hall with the other kitchen girls," Mrs. Grimwald went on, her voice taking on the tone of someone reciting rules to a prisoner. "Rising bell at four in the morning, work until nine at night, one meal at midday and kitchen scraps for your supper if your work satisfies me. One half-day liberty each month, provided your duties are completed to my satisfaction."

She paused at the scullery door, her pale eyes glittering with something that might have been satisfaction. "And child—let there be no mistake about your position here. You are not a guest, nor a ward of His Lordship's charity. You are a servant, and the daughter of a thief besides. The other staff will treat you accordingly, and you will accept their judgment without complaint. Any attempt to trade on past acquaintance with this household will be met with immediate dismissal."

With that cheerful pronouncement, Mrs. Grimwald swept from the room, leaving Opal standing in the steamy heat of the scullery with nothing but her mother's hidden Bible, her father's mysterious key, and the growing certainty that her childhood had ended forever in the space of a single, terrible night.

Jenny looked up from her scrubbing with something approaching kindness in her tired eyes. "Best get started then," she said quietly. "Mrs. Grimwald don't hold with idle hands, and there's always more pots than hours to clean them."

Opal rolled up her sleeves and knelt beside the great stone sink, plunging her hands into water so hot it made her gasp. As she began to scrub her first pot in what would surely be an endless parade of dirty vessels, she wondered if her father was somewhere safe, and whether he would ever know what had become of the daughter he had been forced to abandon.

The key pressed against her body with each movement, a small reminder that this was not the end of her story—only a harsh and painful beginning.

CHAPTER 3

THE SERVANTS' hall at Ashford Manor held all the warmth and comfort of a tomb. Opal lay on her thin straw mattress, listening to the other kitchen girls' steady breathing and trying to ignore the gnawing ache in her stomach. Six months had passed since that terrible dawn when her world had crumbled, and each day brought fresh reminders of how thoroughly her life had changed.

Her hands, once soft from tending house for her father, were now cracked and bleeding from the harsh lye soap and scalding water that had become her constant companions. Her back ached from bending over the great stone sink for fifteen hours each day, scrubbing pots that seemed to multiply the moment she finished cleaning them. But worse than the physical torment was the isolation—the other servants treated her as though she carried some contagious disease, crossing themselves when she passed and speaking of her only in whispers that carried words like "thief's spawn" and "bad blood."

Even Jenny, who had shown her initial kindness, now kept her distance after Mrs. Grimwald's harsh reminder that "associating with criminals brings nothing but trouble." Opal ate her meagre meals alone, worked in solitude, and spent her rare moments of rest dreaming of her father's gentle voice and wondering if she would ever feel human warmth again.

The autumn wind rattled the servants' hall windows as Opal finally drifted toward sleep, her body too exhausted to maintain consciousness despite her churning thoughts. She had almost reached the blessed relief of oblivion when urgent whispers from the next bed jarred her awake.

"—heard them talking in the drawing room," Jenny was saying to Mary, one of the housemaids. "Lady Ashford wants her gone before Christmas. Says the sight of her makes the family's meals taste bitter."

"Gone where?" Mary whispered back, her voice carrying more curiosity than concern.

"Manchester. There's factories there that take girls her age, no questions asked about their families. Lady Ashford's already written to one—Blackwood's Cotton Mill. They pay good money for healthy children, and they ain't particular about references."

Opal's blood turned to ice in her veins. She had heard whispers about the Manchester factories, places where children worked sixteen hours a day in rooms so filled with cotton dust that they could barely breathe. Workers went in young and healthy and came out old and broken, if they came out at all. It was a death sentence disguised as employment.

"When?" Mary's voice carried a note of something that might have been pity.

"Soon as they can arrange it. Lady Ashford wants it done quietly, like. Make it seem like the girl chose to leave for better prospects." Jenny's whisper grew even softer. "Mrs. Grimwald's already been told to stop giving her the good scraps. Let her get thin and desperate, so when they offer Manchester, she'll think it's a blessing."

Mary made a soft sound of sympathy. "Poor little thing. She's had it hard enough already."

"Shh," Jenny warned. "You know what happens to servants who gossip about the family's business. Best we keep our heads down and say nothing."

Their whispers faded into silence, but Opal lay rigid on her mattress, her heart hammering against her ribs. Manchester. The very word seemed to echo in the darkness like a funeral bell. She had perhaps weeks, maybe less, before they shipped her off to die slowly in some fetid factory. Unless...

Unless what? She was twelve years old, alone in the world, with no money and nowhere to run. Even if she could escape the manor, where would she go? Her father was gone, possibly dead for all she knew. Master Griggs might have shown her kindness once, but he dared not cross Lord Ashford openly. She had no other family, no friends beyond these walls who might shelter her.

The next morning brought its usual procession of pots and pans, but Opal's mind was elsewhere as she scrubbed. She had to find a way to escape the fate Lady Ashford planned for her, but how? Lost in desperate planning, she barely noticed when young Master Edmund entered the scullery with a pitcher of water from the morning's hunt.

"Jenny's busy upstairs," he said, setting the pitcher on the wooden table. "Could you wash this when you have a moment?"

Opal looked up, startled to find herself alone with the boy who had shown her that one moment of kindness on her first day. He had grown in the months since then, his shoulders broadening and his voice deepening toward manhood, but his dark eyes still held the same gentle warmth she remembered.

"Of course, Master Edmund," she said quickly, reaching for the pitcher. But her hands, raw from the morning's work, were clumsy with exhaustion. The vessel slipped from her grasp and shattered on the stone floor, sending shards of pottery skittering across the wet flagstones.

"Oh no," Opal gasped, dropping to her knees to gather the pieces. "I'm so sorry, sir. I'll pay for it somehow, I'll—"

"It's only a pitcher," Edmund said gently, kneeling beside her to help collect the fragments. "No harm done."

But there was harm done—Mrs. Grimwald's voice cut through the scullery like a blade as she appeared in the doorway, her pale eyes taking in the scene with obvious displeasure.

"What is the meaning of this?" she demanded, her gaze fixing on Opal with laser intensity. "Destroying His Lordship's property now, are we?"

"It was an accident," Edmund said quickly, rising to his feet. "I startled her, and—"

"An accident," Mrs. Grimwald repeated, her voice dripping with sarcasm. "How convenient. First her father steals from the estate, and now she destroys what little remains." She advanced on Opal, who was still kneeling amongst the pottery shards. "Did you think to cover your clumsiness by batting your eyes at young Master Edmund? Is that the game you're playing?"

"No ma'am," Opal whispered, her cheeks burning with shame. "I would never—"

"Wouldn't you?" Mrs. Grimwald's hand shot out, gripping Opal's chin and forcing her to look up. "You have the look of your father about you—sly and grasping. No doubt you think to worm your way into this family's affections, just as he wormed his way into Master Griggs' trust."

"Mrs. Grimwald," Edmund began, his voice carrying a note of authority despite his youth, "surely you're being too harsh—"

"Master Edmund," the housekeeper said, her tone suddenly respectful but firm, "your mother would be most displeased to learn you've been frequenting the servants' quarters. Perhaps you should return to your studies while I deal with this... situation."

Edmund looked as though he wanted to argue, but the weight of propriety and family expectation was too strong. He cast one last sympathetic glance at Opal, then left the scullery with obvious reluctance.

The moment he was gone, Mrs. Grimwald's mask of respectful service fell away, revealing the cold cruelty beneath. "So," she said softly, her grip tightening on Opal's chin, "you think to seduce the young master with your pretty looks and pitiful circumstances? You think to rise above your station through feminine wiles?"

"No ma'am," Opal said again, tears starting to stream down her cheeks. "I never meant—"

"Of course you meant it," Mrs. Grimwald cut her off. "It's in your blood—the cunning, the deceit, the grasping for what doesn't belong to you. Your father was the same, charming his way into positions of trust before revealing his true nature."

She released Opal's chin with a sharp push that sent the girl sprawling backwards into the pottery shards. Pain lanced through Opal's palm as a sharp edge cut deep, blood welling up to stain her apron.

"Since you seem to have such difficulty keeping track of His Lordship's property," Mrs. Grimwald continued, her voice deadly calm, "perhaps a reminder of your place is in order. You'll work without meals for the next three days—bread and water only, and precious little of that. And you'll spend your nights in the coal cellar, where the rats can keep you company and remind you of what becomes of thieves and seducers."

The coal cellar. Opal's stomach clenched with terror. She had glimpsed it once during her early days at the manor—a windowless stone chamber beneath the kitchen where sacks of coal were stored during the winter months. It was said to be crawling with rats and so cold that water froze in buckets left there overnight.

"Please," Opal whispered, cradling her bleeding hand against her chest. "Please, I'll do anything. I'll work harder, I'll—"

"You'll do exactly as you're told," Mrs. Grimwald said with satisfaction. "And perhaps next time you'll think twice before trying to bewitch your betters with false tears and pretty smiles."

That evening, as the other servants settled into their beds with full bellies and warm blankets, Opal was marched down to the coal cellar with nothing but her thin dress and the key still hidden beneath her bodice. Mrs. Grimwald locked the heavy door behind her, leaving Opal in a darkness so complete it seemed to have physical weight.

The cellar was everything she had feared and worse. The air was thick with coal dust that made her cough and wheeze, and the stone walls wept moisture that soaked through her dress within hours. Rats scurried in the shadows, their eyes gleaming like tiny stars in the blackness, and more than once she felt their whiskers brush against her ankles as they investigated this new addition to their domain.

But worse than the physical discomfort was the spiritual anguish. Alone in the dark with nothing but her thoughts for company, Opal found herself questioning everything she had believed about justice and goodness. Where was God in all this suffering? Where was the divine protection her mother had promised would come to those who lived righteously? Her father had been the most honest man she knew, yet he was branded a thief and driven from his home. She had done nothing but try to survive, yet she was treated like a criminal.

By the second night, fever had set in from the infected cut on her palm and the constant chill. Opal drifted in and out of delirium, sometimes talking to her mother as though she were still alive, sometimes pleading with her absent father to come rescue her from this nightmare. She barely noticed when the cellar door opened and closed again, too lost in fever dreams to register the footsteps on the stone floor.

It was the touch of a cool hand on her forehead that brought her back to awareness. Someone was kneeling beside her in the darkness, and by the faint light seeping under the door, she could just make out Edmund's worried face hovering above her.

"Dear God," he whispered, his voice filled with horror. "You're still burning with fever."

"Master Edmund?" Opal's voice was barely a croak, her throat raw from coughing. "You shouldn't... Mrs. Grimwald said..."

"Mrs. Grimwald is a cruel old witch," Edmund said fiercely, pressing something cool and wet against Opal's burning forehead. "I checked down here earlier. I've brought you water and some bread. And this—" He pressed a small glass vial into her trembling hands. "It's laudanum from my mother's medicine chest. Just a few drops will help with the fever."

Opal wanted to protest that she couldn't take medicine meant for Lady Ashford, that Edmund would be in terrible trouble if discovered, but the fever had stolen her strength for argument. She allowed him to help her sit up and take a few precious sips of water, each drop feeling like salvation in her parched throat.

"Why?" she whispered when she could speak again. "Why are you helping me?"

Edmund was quiet for a long moment, his hand still cool against her fevered brow. "Because it's right," he said finally.

"Because you're suffering for crimes you didn't commit, and because..." He hesitated, then continued in a rush. "Because I see how the others treat you, and it makes me ashamed of my family's name."

"Your father says my father was a thief," Opal said, testing the words like a question.

"My father says many things," Edmund replied carefully. "But I remember your father, Opal. I remember how he always tipped his cap when we passed in the village, how he never failed to thank Master Griggs for fair payment, how he mended the church gate without being asked because he said it was a Christian duty. That doesn't sound like a thief to me."

His words were like balm to Opal's wounded spirit. For six months, she had endured constant reminders that she was the daughter of a criminal, until she had almost begun to believe it herself. To hear someone speak of Samuel Hartwell's goodness, to know that not everyone had forgotten his true character, filled her with a warmth that had nothing to do with fever.

"But what can I do?" she whispered. "Lady Ashford wants to send me to Manchester, to the factories. Mrs. Grimwald means to starve me until I'm grateful for the chance to leave."

Edmund's face darkened with anger. "Manchester? Those death traps? Mother can't seriously mean to—" He stopped himself, perhaps realising he was speaking treason against his own family. "We'll find another way," he said firmly. "I won't let them send you to die in some factory."

"H-how?" Opal asked, and even as she spoke, she felt a dangerous flutter of hope in her chest.

"I don't know yet," Edmund admitted. "But I'll think of something. In the meantime, you must get well. Can you manage a bit of this bread?"

The bread was fine white flour, soft and sweet—food meant for the family table, not the servants' hall. Opal knew Edmund was risking severe punishment by bringing it to her, but she was too hungry and weak to refuse. She ate slowly, savouring each bite while Edmund kept watch at the door.

"I have to go," he said reluctantly when the bread was finished. "Father expects me at breakfast, and if I'm late, he'll ask questions. But I'll come back tomorrow night, I promise."

"Master Edmund," Opal called softly as he prepared to leave. "Thank you. For believing in my father's innocence, for... for seeing me as more than just a thief's daughter."

Edmund paused at the door, his hand on the heavy latch. "You're not a thief's daughter, Opal," he said quietly. "You're a brave girl who's endured more than anyone should have to bear. And someday, I promise you, the truth will come to light."

He slipped away into the darkness, leaving Opal alone once more. But now the cellar didn't seem quite so cold, the rats

quite so threatening. Someone believed in her father's innocence. Someone saw her as worthy of kindness and protection. It wasn't much, perhaps, but it was enough to kindle a
small flame of hope in her heart.

The next morning, Mrs. Grimwald found Opal sitting upright
instead of collapsed in delirium, her fever broken and her eyes
clear. The housekeeper's face tightened with disappointment,
as though Opal's recovery was a personal affront.

"So," she said coldly, "you've decided to rejoin the living. How
unfortunate. I was beginning to hope we might be spared the
trouble of disposing of you properly."

But even Mrs. Grimwald's cruelty couldn't dampen Opal's
renewed spirits. Edmund's visit had reminded her that she
was not entirely alone in the world, that there were still
people capable of seeing past the lies and accusations to the
truth beneath. And more than that, his words had rekindled
something she had almost forgotten—pride in her father's
memory and determination to prove his innocence.

As she returned to her endless rounds of pot-scrubbing and
floor-mopping, Opal found herself thinking not of escape or
survival, but of justice. Somewhere out there, the truth was
waiting to be discovered. Her father had given her a key for a
reason, had spoken of evidence that might someday clear his
name. Perhaps it was time to stop simply enduring her fate
and start fighting to change it.

The key pressed against her heart as she worked, its metal warmed by her body heat and her growing resolve. Whatever Lord Ashford had done, whatever crimes he had committed and blamed on Samuel Hartwell, Opal would find a way to expose them. She owed that much to her father's memory, to her own future, and to the young man who had risked everything to show her kindness in her darkest hour.

Mrs. Grimwald could lock her in cellars, starve her, work her until her hands bled—but she could not break the spirit that Samuel Hartwell had forged in his daughter. Opal was more than just a thief's daughter or a servant to be discarded. She was her father's child, and she would prove worthy of his trust, no matter how long it took or what dangers she had to face.

The game was far from over. It was only just beginning.

CHAPTER 4

THE FIRST FROST of December painted delicate patterns on the scullery windows as Opal worked her way through the morning's endless stack of copper pots. Three years had passed since that terrible night when her father fled into the darkness, and in that time, she had grown from a frightened child into a young woman of fifteen, though few would recognise the transformation beneath her servant's garb and work-worn hands. Somehow, she had never been sent to Manchester, and though he had never told her so, she was sure it was because of the kindness of the young master.

The kitchen hummed with unusual activity as Cook and her assistants prepared for the Christmas feast still weeks away. Great wheels of cheese arrived daily from the estate's dairy, along with barrels of ale and wine that would grace the Ashford table during the holiday season. The very air seemed charged with anticipation—though not, Opal reflected bitterly, the sort that filled her with joy.

"Mind that pudding basin, girl," Cook snapped as Opal reached for a particularly large vessel. "That's for the Christmas pudding mixture, and it'll need to be spotless. Lady Ashford's expecting guests from London for the holidays, and everything must be perfect."

Opal nodded silently, though the mention of Christmas guests made her stomach clench with anxiety. More guests meant more work, more opportunities for mistakes, and more chances for Mrs. Grimwald to find fault with her performance. The housekeeper had grown increasingly sharp-tempered as winter approached, as though the approaching holiday season only heightened her natural cruelty.

But there had been small mercies too. Edmund's clandestine visits to the coal cellar three years ago had marked the beginning of an unlikely friendship that had sustained them both through the intervening years. He was twenty now, returned from university with broader shoulders and a deeper voice, but his eyes still held the same warmth that had first kindled hope in Opal's heart during her darkest hour.

Their meetings had necessarily become more careful as Edmund grew into manhood and Opal into young womanhood. Where once he might slip her an apple or a bit of bread without causing comment, now such gestures carried implications that could destroy them both. Yet somehow, they managed to find moments—a whispered conversation in the empty stillroom, a brief encounter in the manor's extensive gardens during her rare hours of liberty, always careful to maintain the fiction of master and servant should anyone observe them.

It was during one such meeting, on a crisp December afternoon when the Christmas preparations had granted her an unexpected hour of freedom, that Edmund found her reading in the abandoned mill on the estate grounds. She looked up from the slim book in her lap—a collection of poetry he had given her months earlier—to find him approaching through the frost-silvered grass.

"I wondered if I might find you here," he said, settling beside her on the old millstone that served as her favourite seat. "You've been avoiding the usual places."

"Mrs. Grimwald has been watching me more closely," Opal replied, closing the book carefully and smoothing its worn cover. "She seems to suspect something, though I can't imagine what."

Edmund's expression darkened. "She suspects you're growing too pretty to remain safely invisible," he said bluntly. "I've heard her talking to Mother about your... development."

Heat flooded Opal's cheeks at his words. She was indeed no longer the scrawny child who had arrived at the manor, though she did her best to disguise the changes beneath loose clothing and severe hairstyles. Her figure had filled out despite the meagre servant's rations, and her face had lost its childish roundness, revealing the fine bone structure she had inherited from her mother.

"What did they say?" she asked, though she dreaded the answer.

"That you're becoming a distraction to the male servants, and that something must be done before you cause trouble." Edmund's jaw tightened with anger. "Mother suggested it might be time to find you employment elsewhere—somewhere your presence wouldn't be so... problematic."

The old fear rose in Opal's throat like bile. "Manchester?"

"I won't let that happen," Edmund said fiercely, reaching for her hand before stopping himself. Even here, in this remote corner of the estate, they couldn't risk such intimacy. "I've been thinking, Opal. Perhaps it's time you had some... protection. A position where your virtue would be safeguarded."

"What sort of position?" Opal asked, though something in his tone made her wary.

Edmund looked uncomfortable, his gaze fixed on the frozen ground between his boots. "There are families who seek companions for their daughters—respectable positions in good households. The pay is modest, but you'd have your own room, proper meals, and most importantly, you'd be treated as something more than a servant."

"And how would I obtain such a position without references?" Opal asked quietly. "Mrs. Grimwald would hardly write me a glowing recommendation, and your parents..." She didn't need to finish the sentence.

"I could arrange it," Edmund said, his words tumbling out in a rush. "I have connections now, friends from university whose families might be persuaded to take you on. You're well-spoken, thanks to your father's teaching and the books I've shared with you. You could pass for a tradesman's daughter easily enough."

Opal studied his face, noting the careful way he avoided meeting her eyes. "There's something you're not telling me."

Edmund sighed, finally looking at her directly. "The position would require you to leave Yorkshire. Permanently. The family I have in mind lives in Bath—far enough from here that there would be no danger of... complications."

The word hung between them like a blade. Complications. He meant their growing feelings for each other, the impossible attraction that had blossomed between master and servant despite every social barrier designed to prevent such disasters.

"You want me to go away," Opal said, her voice carefully neutral though her heart was breaking.

"I want you to be safe," Edmund replied with quiet intensity. "Do you think I don't know what my family is capable of? I've heard the stories, Opal. Servants who became inconvenient have a way of... disappearing. And you've become very inconvenient indeed."

Before Opal could respond, the sound of approaching footsteps made them both freeze. Edmund shot to his feet, moving several yards away from her as though examining the mill's crumbling stonework. Opal hastily shoved the book of poetry beneath a loose stone, her heart hammering as Mrs. Grimwald emerged from the tree line with two stable boys in tow.

"Master Edmund," the housekeeper called, her voice carrying its usual syrupy deference when addressing family members. "Your mother has been looking for you. She wishes to discuss the Christmas arrangements."

"Of course," Edmund replied smoothly, though Opal could see the tension in his shoulders. "I was merely inspecting the old mill. Father mentioned it might be suitable for renovation."

Mrs. Grimwald's pale eyes settled on Opal with unmistakable suspicion. "And you, girl. What business do you have here during working hours?"

"I was sent to gather kindling for the kitchen fires," Opal said, indicating the small bundle of twigs she had hastily collected upon hearing the footsteps. "Cook said the mill wood burns particularly well."

It was a plausible lie—the mill's broken timbers were indeed sometimes salvaged for fuel—but Mrs. Grimwald's expression suggested she wasn't entirely convinced. Her gaze moved between Opal and Edmund as though calculating the distance between them, measuring the probability of impropriety.

"Return to the kitchen immediately," she commanded Opal. "The Christmas puddings require constant attention, and Cook has already complained about your absence."

"Yes, ma'am," Opal replied, gathering her meagre bundle of kindling and hurrying past the group without daring to look back at Edmund.

But she could feel Mrs. Grimwald's eyes boring into her back as she walked away, and she knew with sick certainty that their secret meetings had become too dangerous to continue. Whatever Edmund's intentions regarding the position in Bath, it seemed the decision might soon be taken out of their hands entirely.

The kitchen was indeed in chaos when she returned, with Cook red-faced from shouting orders and kitchen maids scurrying to complete their tasks before the dinner preparations began. The great Christmas puddings sat in their basins like dark, fragrant monuments to holiday excess, filled with expensive ingredients that cost more than most servants earned in a month.

"There you are," Cook snapped as Opal hurried to her station. "Mrs. Grimwald has been by and wants to see you in her office the moment you've finished those pots. And mind you don't keep her waiting—she's in a foul temper already."

Opal's stomach clenched as she attacked the remaining dishes with mechanical efficiency. A summons to Mrs. Grimwald's office rarely brought good news, and after the encounter at the mill, she could guess what had prompted it. Dear Lord, but the woman must have run the other way to get ahead of her with the summons. Perhaps she had finally decided to act on her suspicions, to eliminate the "problem" of Opal's presence before it could cause further complications.

Mrs. Grimwald's office was a shrine to order and control, its shelves lined with household ledgers and its walls decorated with framed lists of rules for proper servant behaviour. The housekeeper sat behind her mahogany desk like a judge preparing to deliver sentence, her steel-grey hair pulled back so severely it seemed to stretch her thin lips into a permanent expression of disapproval.

"Sit," she commanded, indicating a straight-backed chair positioned precisely in front of the desk.

Opal sat, folding her hands in her lap and keeping her eyes downcast as she had learned to do during these uncomfortable interviews. Whatever was coming, showing defiance would only make it worse.

"Three years," Mrs. Grimwald began, her voice carrying the weight of accumulated grievances. "Three years you've been in this house, eating our food, wearing our livery, sleeping under our roof. And what have we received in return?"

It was clearly a rhetorical question, but Opal felt compelled to answer anyway. "I've tried to do my duties to your satisfaction, ma'am."

"Have you?" Mrs. Grimwald's laugh was like breaking glass. "Then perhaps you can explain why I continue to receive complaints about your behaviour? Why the male servants seem so distracted when you're about? Why you're so often found in places where you have no business being?"

"I don't know, ma'am," Opal replied truthfully. She had always been careful to avoid unnecessary contact with the male servants, understanding instinctively that such interactions could only lead to trouble.

"Don't you?" Mrs. Grimwald leaned forward, her pale eyes glittering with malice. "Or perhaps you think yourself too clever to be caught in your schemes? Perhaps you believe your pretty face and innocent manner will protect you from the consequences of your actions?"

The accusations were so far from Opal's reality that she almost laughed—almost, but not quite. She had learned better than to show any emotion beyond humble submission in Mrs. Grimwald's presence.

"I have no schemes, ma'am," she said quietly. "I only wish to work and earn my keep."

"Lies," Mrs. Grimwald hissed, rising from her chair and beginning to pace behind the desk. "You think I don't see how you've positioned yourself? How you've used your father's disgrace to gain sympathy? How you've manipulated certain members of this household into believing you deserve special consideration?"

The reference to "certain members" made Opal's blood run cold. Did Mrs. Grimwald know about Edmund's kindnesses? Had someone seen them together despite their precautions?

"I don't understand what you mean, ma'am," Opal said, though her voice was barely above a whisper.

Mrs. Grimwald stopped pacing and fixed Opal with a stare that seemed to penetrate her very soul. "Christmas is coming," she said, her voice deceptively calm. "A time of year when Christian households are expected to show charity and forgiveness. A time when even the most hardened hearts might be moved to clemency."

She paused, letting the words sink in before continuing. "It would be unfortunate if certain... complications... were to mar the family's holiday celebrations. If whispers of impropriety were to reach the ears of their distinguished guests. Don't you agree?"

"Yes, ma'am," Opal managed, though she wasn't entirely sure what she was agreeing to.

"Good." Mrs. Grimwald's smile was as warm as a viper's kiss. "Then you'll understand why I've taken the liberty of writing to several establishments that might provide more suitable employment for a girl of your... particular circumstances. Places where your natural inclinations would be better contained."

The threat was clear enough, even wrapped in Mrs. Grimwald's flowery language. Manchester, or somewhere equally dreadful. Opal's hands clenched in her lap, her nails digging crescents into her palms as she fought to maintain her composure.

"However," Mrs. Grimwald continued, settling back into her chair with obvious satisfaction, "such arrangements take time to finalise. In the meantime, I think it best if your duties were... adjusted. To minimise the potential for further complications."

"What sort of adjustments, ma'am?"

"You'll be moved from the kitchen to the laundry. The work is more isolated, and the conditions are... less conducive to inappropriate socialising." Mrs. Grimwald's smile widened. "I'm sure you'll find it most educational."

Opal's heart sank. The manor's laundry was housed in a separate building, a cold, damp structure where servants toiled over steaming tubs and harsh chemicals. It was considered the worst assignment in the household, reserved for those who had fallen from favour or needed to be taught humility.

"Furthermore," Mrs. Grimwald continued, "your movements about the estate will be strictly monitored. No more wandering during your liberty hours, no more unauthorised visits to remote areas. You'll remain in the servants' quarters when not actively working, where proper supervision can be maintained."

"Yes, ma'am," Opal said, because there was nothing else she could say.

"Excellent." Mrs. Grimwald made a note in one of her ledgers. "You'll begin your new duties tomorrow morning. I trust we understand each other?"

"Yes, ma'am."

"Then you're dismissed. And remember—Christmas can be a time for reflection on one's sins and shortcomings. I suggest you use this opportunity to contemplate the wisdom of accepting whatever future Providence sees fit to provide."

Opal rose from her chair on unsteady legs, curtseyed briefly, and made her escape from the stifling atmosphere of Mrs. Grimwald's office. But even as she hurried back toward the servants' quarters, her mind was racing with possibilities she had never seriously considered before.

Edmund had spoken of protection, of positions in distant households where she might find safety and respectability. Perhaps it was time to stop simply enduring her fate and start taking action to change it. Mrs. Grimwald clearly intended to make her remaining time at the manor as miserable as possible before disposing of her entirely. But what if Opal didn't wait for that disposal? What if she took Edmund up on his offer and disappeared before Mrs. Grimwald could complete her schemes?

It would mean leaving behind the only home she had known for three years, abandoning any hope of discovering the truth about her father's innocence. But it would also mean survival, and the possibility of building a life somewhere beyond the reach of Lord Ashford's influence.

As she climbed the narrow stairs to the servants' quarters, Opal's hand unconsciously moved to her chest, where her father's mysterious key still rested against her heart. For three years she had kept it hidden, waiting for some sign of what it might unlock. Perhaps it was time to stop waiting and start searching for answers—even if that search led her far from everything she had ever known.

Christmas was approaching with its promises of peace and goodwill toward men. But for Opal, it seemed more likely to bring a reckoning that would determine the entire course of her future. Whatever happened, she would face it with the courage her father had instilled in her, and the strength she had earned through three years of surviving the impossible.

The key pressed against her heart as she settled into her narrow bed, its weight a reminder that some secrets were worth preserving, no matter what the cost. Tomorrow would bring new challenges, new humiliations, and new threats to her already precarious position. But tonight, she would allow herself to dream of a future where her father's innocence was proven, where justice finally prevailed, and where the truth was stronger than all the lies that had shaped her world.

Outside her small window, the first snow of December began to fall, dusting the manor grounds with pristine white that would soon be trampled into grey slush by the boots of servants and horses. But for now, in the soft light of the winter moon, everything looked clean and new and full of possibility.

Perhaps, Opal thought as she drifted toward sleep, that was what Christmas truly offered—not the gaudy celebrations of the wealthy, but the quiet hope that even in the darkest of winters, spring would eventually come again.

PART II

CHAPTER 5

THE LAUNDRY PROVED to be everything Mrs. Grimwald had promised and worse. Housed in a low stone building separated from the main manor by a courtyard that trapped the December wind like a funnel, it was a realm of perpetual dampness where the air hung thick with steam and the acrid smell of lye soap. Opal's hands, already roughened by years of scullery work, soon developed new layers of calluses from wrestling wet linens through the wooden mangles and hauling endless buckets of water from the well.

The work began before dawn and continued until long after dark, with only the briefest pause for a midday meal of thin gruel and stale bread. The other laundry workers were a grim lot—older women whose spirits had been broken by years of thankless toil, and younger girls who had fallen from favour in the main house. They spoke little and smiled less, their

conversation limited to complaints about the cold, the dampness, and the impossible standards Mrs. Grimwald demanded.

"She's trying to break you," confided Martha, a thin woman of
perhaps forty whose cough had worsened noticeably since
Opal's arrival. "Seen it before with girls who get above themselves. Work them until they beg for whatever escape she
offers, then act like she's doing them a kindness."

Opal nodded as she fed another load of sheets through the
mangle, her arms aching from the repetitive motion. Two
weeks had passed since her banishment to the laundry, and
already she could feel her strength ebbing away under the
relentless physical demands. Her hands were permanently
stained with soap and chemicals, her back constantly ached
from bending over the washing tubs, and the damp cold had
settled into her bones like a living thing.

Worse than the physical hardship was the isolation. Cut off
from the main house's bustle and gossip, she heard nothing of
Edmund or his family's Christmas preparations. Mrs.
Grimwald's restrictions on her movements meant she was
confined to the laundry building and the servants' quarters,
with no opportunity for the clandestine meetings that had
sustained her spirits for so long. She might as well have been
imprisoned in a tower for all the contact she had with the
outside world.

The Christmas season proceeded around her like a distant
dream. Occasionally she glimpsed delivery wagons bringing

exotic foods and fine wines to the manor, heard snatches of carol singing from the village church carried on the wind, caught the sweet scent of puddings and mince pies drifting from the kitchen. But these reminders of festive joy only emphasized how completely she had been excluded from the warmth and comfort that Christmas should bring.

It was during one of her rare moments of rest—a brief respite while Martha tended the fire that heated the washing water— that Opal noticed something unusual about the stone wall behind the largest washing tub. The mortar between two blocks seemed looser than the rest, as though it had been recently disturbed. Curious despite her exhaustion, she knelt and worked her fingers into the crack, feeling around the edges of the stone.

To her amazement, the block shifted slightly under pressure. Heart hammering with sudden excitement, Opal glanced around to ensure she was unobserved, then carefully worked the stone loose enough to peer behind it. What she saw made her gasp with shock.

A folded piece of paper, crumpled and bearing her name in her father's familiar handwriting.

With trembling fingers, she extracted the paper and quickly pushed the stone back into place, tucking the precious docu-ment inside her bodice next to the key that had been her only link to her father for three long years. Whatever the paper contained, it would have to wait until she could examine it safely, away from the prying eyes of her fellow workers.

That evening, pleading exhaustion, Opal retired early to the servants' quarters and waited until the other girls were deeply asleep before lighting a precious stub of candle. By its flickering light, she unfolded her father's message with hands that shook from more than cold.

My dearest daughter, the letter began, *if you are reading this, then you have found your way to the truth I have been so desperately trying to preserve. The key I gave you opens a chamber in the old mill —look for the stone marked with our family's sign, the three interlocked circles your mother carved there during our courtship. Inside you will find evidence of Lord Ashford's crimes, proof that I am innocent of the charges laid against me.*

But Opal, my brave girl, you must be careful. Lord Ashford is more dangerous than you know, and he will kill without hesitation to protect his secrets. Trust no one completely, save perhaps the boy who has shown you kindness. His heart is good, though his loyalty may be divided when the truth comes to light.

I have been watching you from afar, my child, and I am so proud of the woman you are becoming. Soon I may be able to reveal myself fully, but for now I must remain hidden. The sickness grows worse each day, and I fear I may not live to see you fully vindicated. If that happens, you must use what I have gathered to clear our family name, even if it means trusting those who should be our enemies.

All my love, until we meet again—Your devoted father

The letter was dated only one and a half weeks earlier.

Opal's heart nearly stopped as the implications crashed over her. Her father was alive—had been alive this whole time, watching her suffer while remaining hidden. The knowledge filled her with a complex mixture of joy, relief, and burning anger. How could he have left her to endure three years of torment when he was so close by? How could he have watched Mrs. Grimwald's cruelties without intervening?

But beneath the anger was desperate hope. If Samuel was still alive, if he truly had evidence of Lord Ashford's crimes, then perhaps there was still a chance for justice. Perhaps her long nightmare might finally be nearing its end.

The next morning brought the first heavy snowfall of December, blanketing the manor grounds in pristine white that would have been beautiful under other circumstances. But for Opal, struggling through her duties while her mind raced with plans for escape, the snow only added another layer of misery to her already challenging existence. The laundry building's windows were soon blocked with drifts, and the cold seeped through every crack and crevice until even the steam from the washing tubs couldn't provide adequate warmth.

It was during the midday meal break, as the other workers huddled around the small fire and complained about the weather, that Opal made her move. Claiming she needed to visit the privy, she slipped out of the laundry building and into the swirling snow. The walk to the old mill would normally take twenty minutes, but the drifts and limited visibility made progress treacherous. More than once she lost her way entirely, forced to backtrack and search for familiar landmarks buried under the relentless white.

By the time she reached the mill, her feet were numb with cold, and her thin shawl was sodden with snow. But desperation drove her forward as she searched the ancient stones for the family mark her father had mentioned. Finally, near the base of the eastern wall, she found it—three interlocked circles carved into the weathered stone, so faded they were barely visible.

The key her father had given her three years ago fit perfectly into a hidden lock concealed behind the carved stone. With a grinding of ancient metal, a section of the wall swung inward to reveal a narrow chamber barely large enough for a man to stand upright. And there, huddled on a pile of mouldering blankets, was Samuel Hartwell himself.

Opal's first impulse was to cry out with joy, but the sound died in her throat as she took in her father's appearance. The robust, cheerful man who had raised her with such gentle care was gone, replaced by a gaunt scarecrow whose hollow cheeks and sunken eyes spoke of terrible suffering. His once-strong hands shook with more than cold as he looked up at her, and when he coughed, she could see flecks of blood on his lips.

"Papa," she whispered, dropping to her knees beside him and

gathering his frail body into her arms. "Oh Papa, what have they done to you?"

"My brave girl," Samuel managed between coughing fits, his voice barely above a whisper. "I knew you would find me eventually. I've been... waiting so long to see you again."

"But Papa, you've been locked inside. How have you—" she started, but he raised a thin arm to stop her.

"I can get out from inside." His voice was so weak. "And I have the second key. Lately, though, it's been hard."

The joy of reunion was tempered by the obvious gravity of his condition. Even to Opal's untrained eye, it was clear that her father was dying. The consumption that had already been evident in his letter had progressed to its final stages, leaving him little more than skin and bones wrapped in threadbare clothing.

"Why didn't you come to me sooner?" Opal asked, tears streaming down her cheeks as she held him close. "I could have helped you, cared for you—"

"Too dangerous," Samuel interrupted, gripping her hands with surprising strength. "Ashford has men watching... always watching. If he knew I was still alive, still gathering evidence..." Another coughing fit seized him, leaving him gasping for breath.

"What evidence, Papa? Your letter mentioned proof of his crimes."

With obvious effort, Samuel pointed toward a small wooden chest hidden beneath the blankets. "Everything is there. Documents, witness statements from other villages where he's committed crimes. The weapon he used to kill that poor merchant—I managed to retrieve it from where he hid it."

Opal opened the chest with shaking hands, revealing a collection of papers covered in her father's careful handwriting, along with what appeared to be a bloodstained knife wrapped in oiled cloth. The sight of the weapon made her stomach lurch, but she forced herself to examine the documents in the flickering candlelight. They painted a picture of Lord Ashford as a killer who had been murdering travellers for their valuables for years, always managing to blame his crimes on convenient scapegoats.

"He's done this before," Opal breathed, looking up at her father in horror.

"Many times," Samuel confirmed weakly. "I spent months tracking down the families of his other victims, gathering their stories. But it's all circumstantial, child. Without witnesses to his actual crimes..."

"But you witnessed him kill the merchant," Opal protested. "Surely your testimony—"

Samuel's bitter laugh turned into another coughing fit. "The word of a fugitive thief against a lord of the realm? They'd hang me before I could finish speaking." He gripped her hands tighter. "But you, my dear one. You've lived in his house, seen his true nature. If you could find a way to make others see..."

"How, Papa? No one listens to servants, especially not the daughter of an accused thief."

"The boy," Samuel said urgently. "Young Master Edmund. He has a good heart—I've watched him show you kindness when he thought no one was looking. He has the authority to demand a proper investigation, if only he could be convinced..."

"You want me to tell Edmund everything?" Opal asked, her mind reeling at the implications. "But what if he chooses loyalty to his family over justice?"

"Then we are lost," Samuel admitted. "But what choice do we have? I'm dying, child. This consumption will claim me within days, perhaps hours. If justice is to be done, it must be soon."

As if to emphasize his words, another violent coughing fit seized him, this one bringing up more blood than before. Opal held him as his body shook with the effort to breathe, her tears falling freely as she realized how little time they had left together.

"Don't weep for me, my brave girl," Samuel whispered when the fit passed. "I've had three years to prepare for this moment. My only regret is the suffering you've endured because of my choices."

"Your choices?" Opal pulled back to look at him in confusion. "Papa, you did nothing wrong. You witnessed a murder and were framed for theft."

"I could have taken you with me that night," Samuel said, his eyes bright with fever and regret. "Could have found a way to keep you safe while I gathered evidence. Instead, I left you to face Ashford's wrath alone, told myself it was for your own protection."

"It was for my protection," Opal insisted fiercely. "If we had fled together, they would have hunted us both. This way, at least one of us will survive long enough to seek justice."

Samuel smiled at her words, and for a moment she caught a glimpse of the loving father she remembered. "You always were wiser than your years, my dear one. Your mother would be so proud of the woman you've become."

They spent the next hour in quiet conversation as Samuel shared the details of his hidden life over the past three years. He had survived by stealing food from the manor's stores, by finding shelter in abandoned buildings and caves throughout the estate—until he'd come to this final hiding place, the one he had known well for he had been storing up evidence there from even before his escape. He had lived a desperate, lonely existence, sustained only by love for his daughter and determination to clear their family name.

"The key you carry," he said as his strength began to visibly fade, "there's more it can unlock. Hidden compartments in this chamber, other evidence caches I've established. Promise me you'll use them wisely."

"I promise, Papa," Opal whispered, clutching his cold hands in hers.

"And promise me something else," Samuel continued, his voice growing weaker. "Don't let hatred consume you as it nearly consumed me. Ashford is evil, yes, but there are good people in this world too. Young Edmund, perhaps others. Don't close your heart to them because of one man's crimes."

"I promise," Opal repeated, though she wasn't sure how she could keep such a vow.

"And Opal..." He was struggling greatly now. "Wh-when I die, you'll have to leave me in one of the ... chambers. It will seal me up tightly."

She began to weep, but he stopped her. "No, my love. Don't cry. It... it will be all right. Seal me up. Let me g-go..."

As the short winter day began to fade, Samuel's breathing grew increasingly laboured. Opal held him close, whispering stories of her life at the manor, sharing memories of happier times before their world had crumbled. When the church bells in the village chimed six o'clock, marking the end of another day, Samuel Hartwell drew his last breath in his daughter's arms.

Opal sat in the growing darkness as the candle wore down to a stub, holding her father's still form and weeping for all they had lost, all they would never have together. When her tears were finally spent, she gently closed his eyes. She stood, crouching, as that was all that was possible, and found another chamber, just as her father had said. With great effort, she dragged his body into it and arranged him with as much dignity as the cramped chamber allowed. There could be no proper funeral, no ceremony to mark his passing—Lord Ashford's reach was too long, his power too absolute for such gestures.

Instead, she would have to become his monument, his voice crying out for justice from beyond the grave.

This chamber was now Samuel's grave. She wrapped his body in the cleanest blanket she could find and slipped from the chamber, securing the heavy stone closure. It clicked in place, and she knew the key she held would never be used on it again. After leaving the larger area, she arranged the stone with the pattern their family had always used—three interlocked circles representing the eternal bonds of love. It was poor enough burial site for such a good man, but it was all she could manage.

By the time she finished, full darkness had fallen, and the snow had begun again in earnest. Opal made her way back to the laundry building like a sleepwalker, carrying the wooden box, hiding it beneath her cloak as best he could, her body moving automatically while her mind struggled to process everything that had happened. She had found her father only to lose him again within hours, but now she possessed the evidence needed to clear his name and expose Lord Ashford's crimes.

The question was whether she could find the courage to use it.

Martha looked up from her mending as Opal slipped back into the servants' quarters, her sharp eyes taking in the girl's dishevelled appearance and obvious distress.

"Where were you?" she cried. "I had to cover for you. I nearly got whipped."

Opal blinked. "I-I'm sorry. What did you say?"

"I said you was sick. Where *were* you?"

"I tried to visit ... a ... relative."

"Well, it nearly cost me my dinner. Don't you *ever* do that again. I won't cover for you next time."

"I'm sorry. Thank you. Truly. Thank you."

"You look like you've seen a ghost, child," Martha said softly, mindful of the other sleeping workers. "Everything all right?"

"J-Just the cold," Opal replied, though her voice sounded hollow even to her own ears. "The privy is particularly miserable in this weather. And, and I never found my kin."

Martha's expression suggested she didn't believe the excuse, but she was too tired to press for details. "Well, get yourself warmed up then. And you're going to have to be well tomorrow. But you'd better say you was sick if anyone asks. Mrs. Grimwald wants an early start tomorrow—seems the Christmas guests are arriving sooner than expected, and there's extra linens to be washed."

Christmas guests. Opal had almost forgotten about the approaching holiday amid her family's personal tragedy. But now the mention of visitors sparked an idea so audacious it made her hands tremble. What if her father had been right about Edmund? What if there was a way to use the Christmas season—with its emphasis on truth, justice, and redemption —to finally expose Lord Ashford's crimes?

She would need to be careful, clever, and desperately brave. But as she settled into her narrow bed with her father's evidence hidden beneath her mattress, Opal found herself filled with a grim determination that would have made Samuel proud. The game Lord Ashford had started three years ago was far from over.

The next morning brought news that sent ripples of excitement through the servants' quarters. Lord Ashford's Christmas guests were indeed arriving early—a party of wealthy London merchants and their families who would be staying through Twelfth Night. The manor buzzed with frantic preparations as Cook revised her menus and Mrs. Grimwald terrorized the housemaids into producing levels of cleanliness that bordered on the supernatural.

For Opal, toiling away in the laundry with her father's secrets burning in her heart, the increased activity provided unexpected opportunities. In the chaos of preparation, servants moved more freely between buildings, carrying messages and supplies without the usual strict supervision. If she could find a way to get word to Edmund about what she had discovered...

But approaching him directly would be impossible under the current circumstances. She would need an intermediary, someone who could carry a message without arousing suspicion. As she fed another load of table linens through the mangle, her mind ran through the possibilities.

Jenny, her old friend from the scullery, was too frightened of authority to be trusted with such dangerous information. The housemaids were all thoroughly under Mrs. Grimwald's thumb. But what about the stable boys? They had more freedom of movement, and some of them were known to supplement their wages by carrying messages for the right price.

It was a desperate plan, fraught with risks that could see her transported or worse if discovered. But as she thought of her father's wasted body and dying words, Opal knew she had no choice. Justice had waited three years already—it could wait no longer.

The evidence was in her hands, hidden in her chamber. The weapon, the witness statements, the careful documentation of

Lord Ashford's pattern of murder and deception. All she needed was someone with the authority and courage to act on it.

Whether that someone was Edmund Ashford remained to be seen. But as the Christmas bells began to ring across the snowy countryside, calling the faithful to celebrate the birth of hope into a dark world, Opal allowed herself to believe that miracles were still possible. Even for the daughter of an accused man who carried the proof of a lord's guilt hidden next to her heart.

CHAPTER 6

THE ARRIVAL of Lord Ashford's Christmas guests transformed the manor into a hive of barely controlled chaos. Carriages rolled up the circular drive throughout the morning, disgorging London's finest merchants and their elaborately dressed families onto the snow-dusted steps. From her position at the laundry building's single grimy window, Opal watched the procession with a mixture of fascination and growing desperation.

Each new arrival represented another layer of protection around the Ashford family, another barrier between her and any hope of justice. How could she possibly approach Edmund when he was surrounded by houseguests, family obligations, and the constant scrutiny that came with playing host to such distinguished visitors?

"Stop gawking and get back to work," Martha called from across the steamy room, though her tone held more amusement than censure. "You'll have plenty of time to watch the toffs when we're done washing their fancy linens."

Opal turned back to her tub of soaking bed sheets, but her mind remained fixed on the problem of reaching Edmund. Three days had passed since her father's death, and with each hour that slipped away, she felt the weight of his final trust pressing more heavily upon her shoulders. Samuel had died believing that justice was possible, that the evidence he had so carefully gathered might finally clear their family name. She could not—would not—let his sacrifice be in vain.

The opportunity she had been praying for came that evening, delivered in the most unlikely form imaginable.

Mrs. Grimwald herself appeared at the laundry building just as the workers were banking their fires for the night, her severe black dress making her appear like a carrion crow against the snow. Behind her trailed a nervous-looking kitchen maid carrying an enormous basket of table linens.

"There's been an incident in the dining room," the housekeeper announced, her voice tight with barely suppressed fury. "Young Master Edmund spilled claret over half the table setting during dinner. These must be washed and pressed immediately—the family cannot dine off stained linen in front of their guests."

Martha stepped forward, wiping her hands on her apron. "Begging your pardon, ma'am, but we've already banked the fires for the night. It'll take hours to get the water hot enough again, and longer still to wash and press everything properly."

Mrs. Grimwald's pale eyes glittered with dangerous intent. "Then you'll work through the night if necessary. Lord Ashford will not tolerate substandard service, particularly not during the Christmas season when appearances matter most."

The kitchen maid set down her heavy basket and fled back toward the main house without waiting to be dismissed. Martha examined the stained linens with the practiced eye of someone who had spent years battling the evidence of aristo-cratic excess.

"This is more than I can manage alone," she said carefully. "Not if you want it done properly and quickly. I'll need at least one more pair of hands."

Mrs. Grimwald's gaze swept the small group of laundry workers before settling on Opal with obvious malice. "Very well. You," she pointed a bony finger at Opal, "will assist with the emergency washing. But mark me well—if so much as a thread is damaged, the cost will come from your hide."

After the housekeeper departed, Martha shook her head grimly as she rekindled the fires. "Emergency washing on Christmas Eve. As if we don't have enough to do already." She glanced at Opal with something approaching sympathy. "Still, at least it gets you out of the regular duties for a night. Small mercies, eh?"

But Opal was barely listening to Martha's complaints. Her mind was racing with the possibilities that had just opened before her. Emergency washing meant she would be working through the night, moving freely between the laundry building and the main house to collect supplies and deliver finished linens. In the controlled chaos of holiday preparations, she might have a chance to reach Edmund without arousing suspicion.

The work itself was backbreaking. The claret stains proved stubborn, requiring multiple applications of salt and lemon juice before they would lift from the fine damask. Each piece had to be carefully scrubbed by hand, then put through the mangle before being hung to dry near the roaring fires. By midnight, the laundry building was stifling hot and thick with steam, but they had made good progress on the most urgent pieces.

"I'll take the first batch up to the house for pressing," Opal volunteered as Martha paused to wipe sweat from her brow. "The pressing room should be empty at this hour."

Martha nodded gratefully. "Aye and check the linen cupboard just in case while you're there. We'll need fresh tablecloths for tomorrow's Christmas dinner if these don't come clean enough."

Opal gathered an armload of damp linens and stepped out into the frigid December night. The contrast between the laundry's oppressive heat and the sharp cold air was shocking, but welcome after hours of breathing steam and chemical fumes. Snow crunched beneath her feet as she made her way across the courtyard, the manor's windows glowing warmly against the winter darkness.

The servants' entrance was unlocked—it had to be, with staff moving constantly to serve the guests—but the corridors beyond were dimly lit and eerily quiet. Most of the family and their visitors would be in the drawing room enjoying after-dinner entertainment, while the senior servants attended their needs. It was the perfect time for clandestine movement, if one was careful and quiet.

Opal made her way to the pressing room, a small chamber adjacent to the housekeeper's office where delicate items received their final preparations. The room contained everything she needed—a heated iron, starch solution, and the pressing boards where wrinkled linens could be restored to perfection. But more importantly, it was located near the main staircase that led to the family's private chambers.

Working quickly but carefully, Opal pressed the first batch of linens while listening intently for sounds of movement in the corridors beyond. The manor's Christmas guests had brought their own servants, creating additional traffic throughout the building as valets and lady's maids attended their employers' needs. If she could time her movements correctly...

The sound of footsteps in the corridor made her freeze, iron suspended over a half-pressed tablecloth. But the steps continued past without pausing, and she heard the distant murmur of voices as someone descended the main staircase. Male voices, speaking in the casual tones of men who believed themselves unobserved.

"—told you that claret was too young to serve," one voice was saying with obvious amusement. "Father's face when you knocked over the decanter was absolutely priceless."

"It wasn't intentional," replied a second voice, and Opal's heart leaped as she recognized Edmund's warm tones. "Though I'll admit the conversation was becoming rather tedious. How many times can one discuss the merits of different shipping routes before one's mind begins to wander?"

The voices were growing closer, and Opal realized the men were heading in her direction. Fighting down panic, she forced herself to continue pressing the tablecloth with steady, practiced movements. If they discovered her here, she would claim to be following Mrs. Grimwald's orders—which was, after all, perfectly true.

"Still," the first voice continued, "you've given the servants quite a lot of extra work. Mrs. Grimwald looked ready to commit murder when she saw the state of those linens."

"Poor girl," Edmund said, and there was genuine concern in his voice. "I hope she doesn't take it out on the laundry staff.

They work hard enough as it is without having to manage my clumsiness."

The voices had stopped just outside the pressing room door. Opal held her breath, praying they would move on, but instead she heard the soft click of a door opening nearby—Edmund's study, if she remembered the manor's layout correctly.

"Nightcap?" the first voice asked.

"Why not," Edmund replied. "Though I should warn you, I'm poor company tonight. Something about this season always makes me melancholy."

"Christmas blues? That's not like you, old man."

"Perhaps. Or perhaps I'm simply growing tired of playing the dutiful son while watching..." Edmund's voice trailed off, as though he had caught himself before saying something indiscreet.

The study door closed, cutting off their conversation. Opal stood frozen for several heartbeats, her mind racing. Edmund was alone with a single companion, probably a university friend or family acquaintance. If she could find a way to get a message to him without the other man noticing...

But how? She could hardly knock on his study door and announce herself. Even if Edmund was willing to listen, the presence of a witness would make such a meeting impossible. Unless...

An idea began to form in her mind, so desperate and dangerous that it made her hands shake. But with her father's evidence burning like a guilty secret in her memory, she knew she had to try something. Waiting for a better opportunity might mean waiting forever.

Moving with exaggerated care to avoid making noise, Opal set down her iron and crept to the pressing room door. The corridor beyond was empty, lit only by a few wall sconces that cast dancing shadows on the panelled walls. Edmund's study was three doors down, its entrance marked by a warm glow seeping beneath the door frame.

Taking a deep breath to steady her nerves, Opal knocked softly on the door—so softly that someone inside would have to strain to hear it.

"Come," Edmund's voice called, sounding mildly puzzled.

Opal knocked again, slightly louder this time, then quickly retreated to the shadows beside a large portrait of some long-dead Ashford ancestor. If her plan worked, Edmund would come to investigate the mysterious knocking, and she would have a chance to catch his attention without his companion noticing.

The study door opened, spilling golden light into the corridor. Edmund stepped out, looking both ways with obvious confusion. He had changed from his dinner clothes into a comfortable smoking jacket, and his dark hair was slightly dishevelled in a way that made him look younger and more approachable.

"Anyone there?" he called softly, then muttered under his breath, "Probably the wind rattling something loose."

As he turned to go back inside, Opal stepped forward just enough to catch the light from the study. "Master Edmund," she whispered, her voice barely audible.

He spun around, his eyes widening with shock as he recognized her. For a moment they simply stared at each other across the dimly lit corridor—he in his gentleman's evening wear, she in her stained work dress with her hair escaping from its severe bun. The gulf between their stations had never seemed wider or more impossible to bridge.

"Opal?" he breathed, glancing quickly back toward his study where his companion waited. "What are you doing here? If Mrs. Grimwald finds you—"

"I must speak with you," she interrupted, stepping further into the light so he could see the desperate urgency in her face. "It's about my father. About the truth."

Edmund's expression grew troubled, conflict warring visibly in his features. "This isn't the time or place—"

"There may not be another chance," Opal pressed, taking another step closer. "Please. Just five minutes. I have something to show you, something that changes everything."

"Edmund?" The voice from the study sounded questioning. "Everything all right out there?"

"Just checking on something," Edmund called back, his eyes never leaving Opal's face. "I'll be right back."

He moved closer to her, lowering his voice to barely above a whisper. "What kind of something?"

From her bodice, Opal carefully extracted a single sheet of paper—one of her father's witness statements, chosen because it contained no information that could directly implicate Samuel if discovered. "Evidence," she said simply, holding it where Edmund could see the careful handwriting. "Proof that my father was innocent, that Lord Ashford—"

"Don't." Edmund's hand shot out to cover hers, pressing the paper back against her chest. "Don't say it aloud. Not here, not where anyone might hear."

But the very fact that he had stopped her from naming his father told Opal everything she needed to know. Edmund suspected something. Perhaps he had always suspected, had been carrying his own doubts and questions about that terrible night three years ago.

"Will you look at it?" she asked, her voice trembling with hope and fear. "Will you at least consider that there might be more to this than you've been told?"

Edmund glanced back toward his study, where his companion was undoubtedly growing curious about the delay. When he looked at Opal again, his face was etched with pain and uncertainty.

"Not now," he said finally. "But... tomorrow night. The family always attends midnight service at the village church, even the guests. The house will be nearly empty except for a few servants on duty."

"Where?" Opal breathed.

"The old mill. Do you know it?"

Opal's heart clenched at the mention of her father's final resting place, but she managed to nod.

"Eleven o'clock," Edmund continued. "I'll find an excuse to stay behind, claim illness or some such. But Opal—" He gripped her hand tightly, his eyes boring into hers. "If this is some sort of trap, if you're working with someone who means my family harm—"

"It's not," she assured him fiercely. "I swear on my mother's grave. All I want is the truth."

"Edmund!" The voice from the study was growing impatient. "That brandy isn't going to drink itself!"

"Coming," he called back, then looked at Opal one last time. "Tomorrow night. And be careful—Mrs. Grimwald has been watching you more closely than usual. She suspects something."

He disappeared back into his study, leaving Opal standing alone in the corridor with her heart hammering against her ribs. She had done it—had managed to arrange a meeting with

Edmund, a chance to present her father's evidence to someone who might have the power to act on it.

But as she made her way back to the pressing room to continue her work, doubts began to creep in. What if Edmund's apparent sympathy was merely a performance designed to draw her into revealing more than she should? What if he was already planning to inform his father about their conversation? What if she was walking into a trap that would see her hanged for treason or worse?

There was no way to know for certain. But as she resumed pressing the Christmas linens that would grace Lord Ashford's holiday table, Opal reminded herself that her father had died believing Edmund could be trusted. Samuel had spent three years watching, gathering evidence, studying the people around him. If he believed young Master Edmund had a good heart, then perhaps that belief was worth the terrible risk she was about to take.

The remaining hours until dawn passed in a blur of washing and pressing and careful planning. When Martha finally declared the emergency linens ready for service, Opal volunteered to deliver them to the main house, earning grateful murmurs from her exhausted colleague. But instead of returning directly to the servants' quarters, she made a detour to her chamber.

Working by the light of a single candle, she carefully selected the most damning pieces of evidence from Samuel's collection

—the bloodstained knife, three witness statements from other villages, and a detailed timeline of Lord Ashford's movements that corresponded with unexplained deaths across the county. It was dangerous to remove so much material from its hiding place, but she needed to present Edmund with proof substantial enough to overcome his natural loyalty to his family.

As she prepared to leave the chamber, Opal paused and took a deep breath. The wind howled outside, and snow continued to fall, but inside her chamber, all was peaceful and still.

"I'm going to do it, Papa," she whispered to the cold stone walls. "Tomorrow night I'm going to trust the boy you believed in, just as you asked me to. Please... please let you have been right about him."

The only answer was the wind and the soft patter of snow, but somehow Opal felt a measure of peace settle over her troubled heart. Whatever happened tomorrow night, she would face it with the courage her father had instilled in her and the strength she had earned through three years of surviving the impossible.

The game Lord Ashford had started with a single act of murder was finally approaching its climax. And this time, Opal would not be playing defense.

⬥

THE NEXT DAY dawned grey and cold, with heavy clouds promising more snow before nightfall. The manor buzzed with holiday preparations as Cook put the finishing touches on the Christmas feast, and the housemaids decorated every available surface with holly and ivy. Even the servants seemed caught up in the festive spirit, their usual drudgery lightened by anticipation of the evening's celebrations.

For Opal, toiling away in the laundry while her stomach churned with nervous anticipation, the day seemed to stretch endlessly. Every hour that passed brought her closer to the meeting that would determine her fate—and possibly her father's vindication. She worked mechanically, her hands moving without conscious thought while her mind rehearsed what she would say to Edmund, how she would present the evidence in a way that might overcome his filial loyalty.

As evening approached and the church bells began to ring across the snowy countryside, calling the faithful to the Christmas service, Opal made her final preparations. The evidence was hidden beneath her heaviest cloak, wrapped in oiled cloth to protect it from the weather. Her father's key hung around her neck on a length of string, warm against her skin with the weight of all it represented.

At half past ten, she slipped away from the servants' quarters and began the treacherous walk to the mill. The snow had indeed resumed, falling more heavily than before, and by the time she reached her destination, her cloak was white with accumulated flakes. But the weather also provided cover, muffling sounds and limiting visibility in case anyone happened to be watching.

The mill stood dark and silent against the winter night, its ancient stones barely visible through the swirling snow. Opal made her way to the site of her father's hidden chamber, her heart hammering as she waited to see if Edmund would keep his promise.

At precisely eleven o'clock, she heard the crunch of footsteps in the snow. A dark figure emerged from the storm, tall and broad-shouldered, moving with the confident stride she recognized even through the limited visibility. Edmund had come, just as he had promised.

Now came the moment of truth—literally. In the next hour, she would either clear her father's name and expose a murderer or condemn herself to whatever fate Lord Ashford deemed appropriate for those who dared to threaten his power.

As Edmund approached the mill, Opal stepped forward to meet him, her father's evidence clutched tightly in her hands and her heart full of desperate hope.

The reckoning had finally come.

CHAPTER 7

EDMUND APPEARED through the swirling snow like a figure from a dream, his dark greatcoat making him nearly invisible against the winter night until he was almost upon her. Snowflakes clung to his hair and shoulders, and his breath formed white clouds in the frigid air as he approached the mill's entrance where Opal waited.

"You came," she breathed, relief flooding through her despite the circumstances.

"I gave my word," Edmund replied quietly, his eyes searching her face in the dim light. "Though I'll admit I've spent the entire day questioning my sanity. If my family discovers I'm meeting secretly with—" He stopped himself, perhaps realizing how his words might sound.

"With the daughter of a thief?" Opal finished for him, her voice steady despite the hurt that lanced through her chest.

Edmund's expression grew pained. "That's not what I meant, and you know it. But the reality is that if we're discovered here together, the consequences for both of us would be... severe."

Opal nodded, understanding all too well the risks they were taking. "Then let's not waste time," she said, producing her father's key and moving toward the hidden entrance. "I found something to show you that will change everything you think you know about that night three years ago. I-I wanted to show you the things here where I found them."

She had expected Edmund to show surprise when the section of wall swung inward to reveal the hidden chamber, but his reaction was more complex—shock, yes, but also something that might have been recognition. As though he had suspected such secrets might exist within his family's domain.

"How long have you known about this place?" he asked as they stepped inside the narrow space.

"Three days," Opal replied, lighting the stub of candle she had brought. "My father left me clues, instructions on where to find him when the time was right."

"Find him?" Edmund's voice sharpened with sudden attention. "Opal, you're speaking as though your father were still alive. But surely—"

"He was alive," Opal interrupted, her voice catching slightly. "Until three days ago, when the consumption finally claimed him. He died in my arms, right here in this chamber where he had been hiding."

The candlelight flickered across Edmund's face, revealing a mixture of shock and something deeper—something that might have been guilt.

"Dear God," he whispered. "All this time, he was so close by? And we never knew, never suspected..."

"Someone suspected," Opal said grimly. "Someone knew he was still alive and still gathering evidence. Why else would your family have been so eager to dispose of me? First the threats of Manchester, then my banishment to the laundry where I could be watched more easily. They were afraid of what I might discover."

Edmund was quiet for a long moment, his gaze moving around the small chamber that had been Samuel's final refuge. When he spoke again, his voice was heavy with conflicted emotion.

"Show me," he said simply. "Show me this evidence you claim changes everything."

With trembling hands, Opal unwrapped the oiled cloth that protected her father's most damning documents. One by one, she laid them out on the rough wooden table Samuel had constructed from mill debris—witness statements from three different villages, each describing unexplained deaths that had occurred shortly after Lord Ashford's visits. A detailed timeline showing the pattern of these deaths over the past decade. And finally, wrapped in a separate cloth, the bloodstained knife that Samuel claimed was the murder weapon.

Edmund examined each document with growing horror, his face growing paler with every page. The witness statements were particularly damning—accounts from innkeepers and stable masters who remembered Lord Ashford's visits, followed invariably by the discovery of dead travellers who had been robbed and killed. In each case, local authorities had blamed bandits or vagrants, never suspecting that the murderer might be the wealthy nobleman who had departed just hours before.

"This timeline," Edmund said, his voice barely above a whisper as he studied his father's movements. "Some of these dates... I remember them. Father claiming urgent business in distant counties, returning home with new funds for estate improvements. I thought nothing of it at the time, but now..."

"Now you see the pattern," Opal said. "Your father has been murdering travellers for their valuables for years, always managing to deflect suspicion onto convenient scapegoats. My father simply had the misfortune to witness one of these crimes."

Edmund set down the timeline with shaking hands. "But this

is all circumstantial evidence. Coincidences and suspicions, nothing that would stand up in a court of law."

"There's more," Opal said, unwrapping the bloodstained knife. "My father managed to retrieve the actual murder weapon from where your father hid it. He witnessed the entire crime, Edmund. He saw Lord Ashford kill Tobias Fletcher for his purse of gold, then plant evidence that horrible night in our cottage to frame him for theft to get rid of him."

The sight of the weapon seemed to affect Edmund more profoundly than all the written evidence combined. He stared at the stained blade with an expression of such anguish that Opal felt a stab of sympathy despite everything his family had done to her.

"I've seen this knife before," he said finally, his voice hollow with realization. "It belongs to Father's collection—antique weapons he keeps in his private study. I used to play with them as a child until he caught me and forbade me from touching them again."

"Then you believe me?" Opal asked, hardly daring to hope.

Edmund was quiet for so long that she began to fear he was rejecting everything she had shown him. When he finally spoke, his words carried the weight of a man whose entire world had just crumbled beneath his feet.

"I believe that my father is a murderer," he said slowly. "And I believe that your father was an innocent man who died for trying to expose the truth. But believing it and being able to act on it are two very different things."

"What do you mean?" Opal asked, though she feared she already knew.

"I mean that I am one man against an entire system designed to protect people like my father," Edmund replied bitterly. "Even if I took this evidence to the magistrate—assuming I could find one not already in Father's pocket—who would believe it? The word of a runaway servant and a dead thief against a lord of the realm?"

"But you're his son," Opal protested. "Your testimony would carry weight—"

"My testimony would be dismissed as the ravings of a son driven mad by guilt or family disputes," Edmund cut her off. "Or worse, I might simply disappear like so many of Father's other problems have disappeared over the years."

The implications of his words sent a chill through Opal that had nothing to do with the winter cold. "You think he would kill his own son?"

"I ... I think my father is capable of anything," Edmund replied grimly. "And I think we have gravely underestimated the danger we're both in simply by having this conversation."

As if summoned by his words, the sound of voices outside the mill made them both freeze. Multiple voices, growing closer, accompanied by the crunch of many feet in the snow.

"—tracks lead this way, my lord," a gruff voice was saying. "Fresh ones, by the look of them."

"Then we have them cornered," came the reply, and Opal's blood turned to ice as she recognized Lord Ashford's cultured tones. "Excellent work, Morrison. I knew that girl would eventually reveal her true purpose."

Edmund's face had gone ashen. "How did they find us?" he whispered.

"Someone must have seen us leave the manor," Opal replied, though even as she spoke, she realized the truth was likely more sinister. "Or someone has been watching me all along, waiting for exactly this moment."

The voices were very close now, just outside the mill proper. Lord Ashford was giving orders in the crisp, authoritative tone of a man accustomed to absolute obedience.

"Surround the building. If they attempt to run, stop them by whatever means necessary. I want this matter resolved quietly and permanently."

Edmund moved swiftly to extinguish their candle, plunging the chamber into complete darkness. In the blackness, Opal felt his hand find hers, squeezing tightly in what might have been reassurance or farewell.

"There may be another way out," she whispered, considering her father's mention of multiple hiding places throughout the chamber. "He said the key could unlock other secrets."

Working by touch alone, she found the wall where her father had mentioned additional compartments. The key that had been her constant companion for three years fit into a second hidden lock, revealing a narrow passage that led deeper into the mill's foundations.

"This way," she breathed, tugging Edmund toward the escape route.

They crawled through the narrow tunnel in complete darkness, the sound of their pursuers growing fainter behind them. The passage was cramped and claustrophobic, forcing them to move on hands and knees through what felt like an eternity of blackness. Just when Opal began to fear they would be trapped underground forever, her groping hands encountered another wall with another hidden lock.

The passage emerged behind a tangle of brambles some fifty yards from the mill, concealed so cleverly that even someone looking directly at it would be unlikely to spot the entrance. They lay in the snow-covered undergrowth, gasping for breath and listening to the sounds of their pursuers searching the mill.

"He knew," Edmund whispered, his voice filled with wonder and grief. "Your father knew they would come for you eventually, so he made sure you were prepared with an escape route."

"He prepared for everything except living long enough to see justice done," Opal replied, her heart heavy. The evidence that might have cleared her father's name was still hidden in the chamber they had just fled, now certainly discovered by Lord Ashford and his men.

"Not everything is lost," Edmund said, pulling something from inside his coat. In the dim moonlight filtering through the clouds, Opal could see he had managed to grab several of the most important documents during their hasty escape. "I have the witness statements and the timeline. Not everything, but enough to prove the pattern exists."

"What good will it do?" Opal asked despairingly. "You said yourself that no one would believe such accusations against your father."

"Perhaps not here, where his influence is absolute," Edmund agreed. "But there are other authorities, other jurisdictions where his power doesn't reach. If we could get this evidence to London, to officials who owe him no loyalty..."

"We?" Opal stared at him through the swirling snow. "Edmund, you can't seriously be considering—"

"I'm considering doing what's right," he cut her off fiercely. "I've spent my entire life benefiting from wealth built on murder and theft. I've lived in comfort while your father wasted away in hiding and you suffered under our roof as punishment for crimes you never committed. How can I do anything else but try to make amends?"

Before Opal could respond, the sound of approaching voices made them both flatten themselves against the frozen ground. Through the brambles, they could see the glow of lanterns as Lord Ashford's search party expanded their hunt beyond the mill itself.

"They found the chamber," Lord Ashford's voice carried clearly in the still night air. "And evidence of recent habitation. The girl has been meeting someone here regularly."

"What are your orders, my lord?" came Morrison's voice. Opal recognized him now as the constable who had helped frame her father three years ago.

"Find them," Lord Ashford replied coldly. "Search every building, every hiding place on the estate. And when you do find them..." There was a pause that carried more menace than any threat. "Well, tragic accidents do happen during winter storms. Hypothermia can be so unpredictable."

The meaning was clear enough. Lord Ashford intended to ensure that neither Opal nor Edmund would survive to tell anyone what they had discovered. The search party began to spread out, their lanterns bobbing like fireflies in the darkness as they methodically examined every possible hiding place.

"We have to get away from the estate," Edmund whispered urgently. "If we stay here, they'll find us eventually."

"Where can we go?" Opal asked. "Your father's influence

extends throughout the county. There's nowhere we'll be safe."

"Then we'll have to go farther," Edmund replied grimly. "London, as I said. We'll take this evidence to officials who can't be bought or intimidated. It's our only chance."

The plan was desperate to the point of being suicidal, but Opal could see no alternative. To remain on the estate meant certain death, either at Lord Ashford's hands or through the more gradual process of starvation and exposure. At least flight offered the possibility, however remote, of eventual justice.

"How do we get to London without money or transport?" she asked practically.

"Leave that to me," Edmund said, his jaw set with determination. "I have friends who would help us, contacts Father doesn't know about. But first we need to get off the estate without being seen."

They began to move carefully through the undergrowth, keeping low and pausing frequently to listen for sounds of pursuit. The snow continued to fall, which was both blessing and curse—it muffled their movements but also left clear tracks that any competent tracker could follow.

Behind them, the search intensified. More lanterns appeared as additional men joined the hunt, and Opal could hear dogs barking in the distance. Lord Ashford was clearly taking no chances on their escape.

"The old quarry," Edmund whispered as they paused beside a stone wall that marked the boundary of the formal gardens. "There's a path that leads down to the road, but it's treacherous in winter. Father's men might not think to check there immediately."

They made their way toward the quarry with agonizing slowness, every step potentially their last if they were discovered. The abandoned stone pit lay at the estate's eastern edge, a relic from decades past when the Ashfords had quarried limestone for their building projects. The path down was little more than a goat track, made doubly dangerous by the accumulated snow and ice.

Halfway down the quarry's steep side, disaster struck. Edmund's foot slipped on a patch of ice, sending him sliding helplessly down the rocky slope. He managed to arrest his fall by grabbing a protruding stone, but not before crying out in pain as his shoulder struck the quarry wall.

The sound echoed across the winter landscape like a gunshot.

"There!" a voice shouted from above. "I heard something from the quarry!"

Lantern light began to move in their direction as the search party redirected toward the sound. Edmund struggled to his feet, his left arm hanging uselessly at his side, his face white with pain.

"Go," he gasped, pushing Opal toward the bottom of the quarry. "Get to the road. Find help."

"I'm not leaving you," Opal replied fiercely, moving to support his injured side.

"You have to. If they catch us both, everything your father died for will be lost forever." Edmund pressed the folded documents into her hands. "Take these to London. Find someone who will listen. Promise me."

Before Opal could argue further, the first of their pursuers appeared at the quarry's rim, his lantern casting wild shadows on the stone walls. More followed quickly, and soon a dozen lights were moving down the treacherous path toward them.

"This way," Opal said, spotting a narrow crevice in the quarry wall that might provide temporary shelter. "We can hide until they pass."

But Edmund was weakening rapidly, his injured shoulder robbing him of the strength needed to navigate the quarry's hazards. As they struggled toward the crevice, Lord Ashford himself appeared at the quarry's edge, his tall figure silhouetted against the snowy sky.

"Surrender now," his voice boomed across the stone amphitheatre, "and I promise your deaths will be quick and merciful. Continue this futile resistance, and I will ensure you both suffer as my other enemies have suffered."

Opal felt Edmund sag against her as the hopelessness of their situation became clear. They were trapped in a stone bowl with no way out except past their pursuers, and Edmund was in no condition to fight or run. But even as despair threatened to overwhelm her, she remembered her father's dying words about not letting hatred consume her, about trusting in the possibility that good people still existed in the world.

Perhaps those good people would find them. Perhaps justice would prevail despite all odds. Or perhaps she and Edmund would die here in this cold stone pit, their secrets buried with them beneath the Christmas snow.

But whatever happened, she would face it with the courage Samuel Hartwell had instilled in his daughter, and the love that had grown between her and the young man who had chosen justice over family loyalty.

The web Lord Ashford had woven to protect his crimes was tightening around them both. Whether they would escape it or be destroyed by it remained to be seen.

But Opal refused to surrender without a fight. Her father's memory—and Edmund's sacrifice—demanded nothing less than her absolute best effort, no matter how impossible the odds might seem.

The game was far from over. And sometimes, even in the darkest hour, miracles could still happen.

CHAPTER 8

THE QUARRY'S stone walls seemed to close in around them as Lord Ashford's men descended like hunting wolves, their lanterns casting grotesque shadows that danced across the limestone. Opal pressed herself against Edmund's uninjured side, feeling his laboured breathing and the tremor of pain that ran through his body with each movement.

"There," she whispered, pointing to a narrow fissure in the quarry wall that was partially concealed by an overhang of stone. "If we can reach it..."

Edmund nodded grimly, though sweat beaded on his forehead despite the bitter cold. His left arm hung uselessly at his side, and each step seemed to cost him tremendous effort. But he pushed forward with the determination of a man who knew that capture meant death—not just for himself, but for the woman he had come to love beyond all reason or propriety.

They reached the fissure just as the first searcher's lantern began to probe their previous hiding spot. The opening was barely wide enough for two people, forcing them to press together in the darkness while their pursuers' voices echoed off the quarry walls.

"Spread out," Lord Ashford commanded from above, his voice carrying the absolute authority of a man accustomed to being obeyed without question. "Check every crevice, every shadow. They cannot have vanished into thin air."

In the cramped confines of their hiding place, Opal was acutely aware of Edmund's body pressed against hers. Despite the circumstances—perhaps because of them—she found herself noticing details that would have escaped her attention in the past: the way his breathing stirred the hair at her temple, the warmth of his chest against her back, the protective way his good arm curved around her waist to shield her from the rough stone.

"Are you badly hurt?" she whispered, her lips so close to his ear that her breath made him shiver.

"I'll live," Edmund replied softly, though she could hear the pain he was trying to conceal. "The shoulder may be dislocated, but it's nothing that can't be mended if we survive long enough."

"When we survive," Opal corrected fiercely. "I didn't endure three years of misery just to die in a quarry pit before seeing justice done."

Edmund's arm tightened around her waist at her words, and she felt rather than saw his smile in the darkness. "Your father would be proud of your determination."

"My father would be furious that I've involved you in this," Opal replied. "He wanted me to trust you, not destroy your life."

"You haven't destroyed anything," Edmund said with quiet intensity. "You've given me the chance to finally do something worthy of the name I bear. For twenty years I've lived on wealth built from murder and theft, never questioning where our fortune truly came from. If I die tonight trying to make amends, at least I'll die with a clear conscience."

A lantern beam swept past their hiding place, close enough that Opal could see the individual pores on Edmund's face in the brief illumination. They held their breath as boots crunched through the snow just yards away, neither daring to move until the searcher had passed.

"There's something I need to tell you," Edmund whispered when they were alone again in the darkness. "In case we don't... in case this is our only chance."

"Don't," Opal interrupted, her heart clenching with sudden fear. "Don't speak as though we're already defeated."

"I've been in love with you for three years," Edmund continued as though she hadn't spoken, his voice low and urgent. "Since that night I found you in the coal cellar, burning with fever and more beautiful in your suffering than any of the pampered society girls my mother parades before me. I've tried to convince myself it was merely pity, or guilt over my family's treatment of you, but I can't lie to myself anymore."

Opal turned in his arms to face him, though in the absolute darkness she could only sense his presence, feel the warmth of his breath on her face. "Edmund..."

"I know it's impossible," he pressed on desperately. "I know that even if we survive this night, there's no future for us together. A lord's son and a servant girl—the world would never accept such a match, and I have nothing to offer you but scandal and disgrace."

"You have yourself," Opal whispered, her own restraint finally crumbling under the weight of emotions she had fought to suppress for so long. "And that's more than anyone else has ever offered me."

In the darkness, their lips found each other with the desperate hunger of two people who might not live to see another dawn. The kiss was everything Opal had dreamed of and feared in equal measure—tender and gentle, filled with the accumulated longing of years of forced separation. When they finally broke apart, both were breathing hard, their hearts racing.

"I love you too," Opal whispered against his lips. "I've loved you since you first showed me kindness when I had nothing and no one. But you're wrong about our future—we'll make one together, somehow, if we survive this night."

"How?" Edmund asked, though his voice carried more hope than despair now. "How can we build a life together when the entire world conspires to keep us apart?"

"The same way my parents did," Opal replied, thinking of the stories Samuel had told her about his courtship of her mother. "They had nothing but love for each other, no wealth or position or family approval. But they found a way to be happy because they refused to let other people's prejudices define their worth."

Another searcher passed close by, his lantern light briefly illuminating their cramped hiding space. This time, however, the intimate atmosphere created by their confessions made the danger seem somehow less threatening. Whatever happened, they would face it together, and that knowledge gave them both strength.

"The search is moving toward the far end of the quarry," Edmund observed as the voices grew more distant. "If we can work our way around to the eastern wall..."

"There's a path there that leads down to the old Roman road," Opal finished, remembering her father's stories about the quarry's history. "But it's treacherous even in daylight, and with your shoulder..."

"We'll manage," Edmund said grimly. "What choice do we have?"

They waited until the searchers were thoroughly occupied with examining the quarry's deeper recesses before emerging from their hiding place. Edmund's face was grey with pain, but he moved with quiet determination as they picked their way across the uneven stone floor toward the eastern wall.

The ancient path carved into the limestone was every bit as dangerous as Opal had feared. Ice from decades of winter freezing and thawing had made the narrow ledge treacherous, and in several places, they were forced to inch along with their backs pressed against the rock face, trusting their lives to handholds that crumbled at the slightest pressure.

Edmund's injured shoulder made the descent a nightmare of barely suppressed agony. More than once he swayed danger-ously, saved only by Opal's quick reflexes and desperate strength. By the time they reached the bottom, both were exhausted and shaking from more than cold.

"We can't stay on the road," Edmund gasped as they emerged onto the old Roman thoroughfare that connected Lord Ashford's estate to the wider world. "Father's men will search it once they realize we've escaped the quarry."

"The forest," Opal suggested, gesturing toward the dark line of trees that bordered the road. "We can follow the road from within the tree line, stay hidden until we're well clear of the estate."

It was a sound plan, but their progress through the snow-laden forest was painfully slow. Edmund's strength was fading visibly, and Opal found herself supporting more and more of his weight as they struggled through drifts that sometimes reached their knees. Behind them, the glow of searchers' lanterns continued to move through the quarry, but so far, their escape route had not been discovered.

"We need shelter," Opal said after they had been walking for perhaps an hour. "Somewhere you can rest, and we can assess how badly you're hurt."

"There's a woodcutter's cottage about a mile ahead," Edmund replied through gritted teeth. "Abandoned for years, but the roof was still sound when I last saw it. If we can reach it..."

The cottage, when they finally found it, was indeed abandoned but still weathertight. The single room contained only a rough stone fireplace and a few pieces of crude furniture, but after hours in the winter wilderness, it seemed like a palace. Opal helped Edmund settle onto a pile of old sacking before examining his shoulder by the light of a stub of candle she found on the mantelpiece.

"It's definitely dislocated," she said, running her fingers gently over the swollen joint. "I'll need to reset it, but it's going to hurt."

"More than it already does?" Edmund asked with a weak attempt at humour.

"Much more, I'm afraid." Opal had assisted her father in treating similar injuries sustained by workers at the smithy, so she knew the procedure. But doing it to someone she loved, knowing the pain she would cause, made her hands shake with reluctance.

"Do it quickly," Edmund said, seeing her hesitation. "The longer we wait, the harder it becomes."

Opal positioned herself carefully, gripped Edmund's arm and shoulder with firm hands, and pulled with swift, decisive force. The joint snapped back into place with an audible pop, and Edmund's strangled cry of pain echoed off the cottage walls. But when she helped him move the arm experimentally, relief flooded his features.

"Better," he said, flexing his fingers cautiously. "Much better. Where did you learn to do that?"

"My father," Opal replied, settling beside him on the makeshift bed. "He said a smithy must know how to mend bones as well as metal, since both break when put under too much strain."

In the flickering candlelight, with danger temporarily held at bay, the cottage felt isolated from the rest of the world. For the first time in years, Opal was alone with someone who truly cared for her, someone who saw her as more than just a servant or an inconvenience to be managed. The realization was both comforting and terrifying.

"What happens now?" she asked, studying Edmund's face in the golden light. "Even if we reach London, even if we find officials willing to listen to our accusations, your father will not simply accept defeat. He'll use every resource at his disposal to destroy us."

"I know," Edmund admitted. "But what else can we do? Live as fugitives for the rest of our lives? Let my father continue harming innocent people while we hide in shadows?"

Opal was quiet for a long moment, considering their options. All of them seemed to lead to either death or a lifetime of exile from everything they had ever known. But perhaps that was a price worth paying for justice—and for love.

"If we do this," she said finally, "if we take this evidence to London and expose your father's crimes, there will be no going back. You'll lose everything—your inheritance, your family, your position in society. You'll be choosing me over all of that."

Edmund was silent for a long moment, and Opal feared what he might say. But then he began speaking.

"Opal, it can be no other way. I chose you the moment I decided to meet you at the mill. Everything else—the money, the title, the social standing—none of it means anything if it's built on innocent blood. I'd rather be a pauper with you than a wealthy murderer's son without you."

The simple honesty of his words broke down the last of Opal's defences. She had spent three years telling herself that their love was impossible, that the gulf between their stations could never be bridged. But here, in this humble cottage with the world arrayed against them, such considerations seemed petty and meaningless.

"I love you," she said again, the words coming easier this time. "Not Master Edmund Ashford, heir to a great estate. Just you —the man who risked everything to help me find the truth."

When he kissed her this time, there was no desperation born of impending doom, only the sweet certainty of two hearts finally acknowledging what had long been evident to both. They held each other close as the candle burned lower, drawing warmth and comfort from their proximity while the winter wind howled around the cottage walls.

"We should rest," Edmund said eventually, though he made no move to release her from his arms. "Tomorrow will bring new challenges, and we'll need our strength."

"Will you hold me while I sleep?" Opal asked, suddenly feeling like the frightened child she had been when this nightmare began. "I've been alone for so long, and tonight..."

"Tonight, you're not alone," Edmund finished softly, gathering her more securely against his chest. "And if I have any say in the matter, you never will be again."

They settled together on the rough bedding, sharing body heat and the profound comfort of human contact after years of isolation and fear. Outside, the storm continued to rage, but within the cottage's walls, all was peaceful and warm.

As sleep finally claimed them both, Opal allowed herself to dream of a future where love was stronger than social convention, where justice prevailed over wealth and power, where two people who had found each other against all odds might be allowed to keep what they had discovered.

It was perhaps an impossible dream, but it was theirs, and that made it precious beyond measure.

❦

THE FIRST GREY light of Christmas morning found them still entwined in sleep, their faces peaceful despite the dangers that surrounded them. But as consciousness returned and reality reasserted itself, they both knew that their respite was over.

Today they would begin the most dangerous journey of their lives, carrying evidence that could destroy one of England's most powerful families. They would travel as fugitives, with limited resources and powerful enemies in pursuit. The odds against their success were overwhelming.

But they would face those odds together, sustained by love and the absolute certainty that their cause was just. Whatever sacrifices lay ahead, whatever prices they might be forced to pay, they would pay them in the service of truth.

Opal touched the key that still hung around her neck—her father's final gift and the symbol of all the secrets that had yet to be revealed. Samuel Hartwell had died believing that justice was possible, that good could triumph over evil if only the right people had the courage to act.

Today, his daughter and the man she loved would test that belief against the full might of Lord Ashford's power. The outcome was far from certain.

PART III

CHAPTER 9

CHRISTMAS MORNING HAD dawned grey and bitter, with fresh snow falling steadily from a leaden sky that seemed to press down upon the abandoned cottage like a suffocating blanket. Opal had awakened first, Edmund's arms still wrapped protectively around her, his breathing deep and even despite their precarious circumstances. For a precious moment, she allowed herself to simply exist in the warmth of his embrace, pretending they were merely in love and had chosen to spend Christmas together rather than fugitives fleeing for their lives.

But reality intruded all too quickly as the sound of distant church bells drifted across the winter landscape, calling the faithful to mass. Lord Ashford would be attending worship with his London guests, playing the role of the devout country gentleman while his men continued searching for the two people who could expose his crimes. The irony was not lost on Opal—a murderer celebrating the birth of Christ while hunting those who sought justice.

"Edmund," she whispered, gently shaking his unharmed shoulder. "We need to go."

Edmund's eyes focused on her face with an expression of such tender devotion that her heart clenched. "For a moment I almost forgot..."

"I know," Opal said softly, brushing a strand of dark hair from his forehead.

Edmund sat up carefully, testing his shoulder with cautious movements. The joint was still tender, but the desperate pain of the previous night had faded to a manageable ache. "You're right, of course. But where can we go? Every inn and lodging house between here and London will be watched."

"Then we don't use inns," Opal replied, having given the matter considerable thought during the long night. "My father spent three years living rough, surviving on his wits and whatever shelter he could find. If he could do it while dying of consumption, surely we can manage for the few days it will take to reach London."

"You want to walk to London?" Edmund asked incredulously. "That's nearly a week's journey on foot, through winter conditions, with no supplies or warm clothing."

"Not walk," Opal corrected, producing a folded paper from her bodice—one of the documents they had salvaged from her father's evidence. "This witness statement mentions a coaching inn called the Golden Lamb, south of here. The innkeeper there provided testimony about your father's visit, which means he's already suspicious of Lord Ashford's activities. He might be willing to help us."

Edmund studied the document with growing understanding. "You think he'll provide us with transport to London?"

"I think he'll listen to our story, especially if we can convince him that bringing Lord Ashford to justice serves his own interests," Opal replied. "Your father has been murdering travellers along these roads for years. An innkeeper who caters to such travellers would have every reason to want him stopped."

It was a desperate plan built on hope and speculation, but it offered more promise than wandering through the winter wilderness with no destination beyond a vague intention of reaching London eventually. Edmund nodded slowly, his expression thoughtful.

"The Golden Lamb," he mused. "I remember Father mentioning it once—said the proprietor was 'impertinent' and suggested we should find other accommodations when traveling that route. At the time I thought he was simply being particular, but now..."

"Now you understand he was avoiding someone who had seen too much," Opal finished. "Someone who might ask uncomfortable questions about the fate of previous guests."

They gathered their few possessions—Edmund's coat, Opal's thin cloak, and the precious documents that represented their only hope of justice—and prepared to venture once more into the hostile world beyond the cottage walls. Before leaving, Edmund insisted on banking the fire and arranging the cottage to look as though it had remained undisturbed, a precaution that might buy them precious time if their pursuers discovered this refuge.

The journey to the Golden Lamb proved every bit as arduous as Opal had feared. The fresh snow made walking treacherous, and they were forced to leave the main roads whenever they spotted travellers in the distance, taking refuge in fields and woodlands until the danger passed. Edmund's injured shoulder limited his ability to help when Opal struggled through the deeper drifts, and more than once they found themselves supporting each other like wounded soldiers retreating from a lost battle.

By afternoon, exhaustion and cold had taken their toll. Edmund's face was grey with fatigue, and Opal could feel her own strength ebbing away despite her determination to press forward. When they finally spotted the Golden Lamb's welcoming smoke rising from chimneys in the distance, both nearly wept with relief.

The inn proved to be a substantial establishment, its timber-framed walls and thatched roof speaking of prosperity and long-established custom. Light glowed warmly from mullioned windows, and the sound of voices and laughter drifted across the snowy courtyard as guests celebrated Christmas Day in comfort and safety.

"How do we approach this?" Edmund asked as they huddled in the shadow of the inn's stable, trying to work up courage for what might prove to be their final gamble. "We can hardly walk through the front door looking like vagabonds and demand an audience with the proprietor."

"We tell the truth," Opal replied simply. "Or at least enough of it to convince him we're genuine. Your father's crimes have touched this place—the innkeeper knows something is wrong, even if he doesn't know exactly what. We give him the missing pieces and hope his conscience compels him to act."

Before Edmund could argue for a more cautious approach, Opal straightened her shoulders and walked boldly toward the inn's main entrance. Whatever reception awaited them, delay would only increase the likelihood of discovery by Lord Ashford's men.

The inn's taproom was warm and crowded, filled with the cheerful bustle of Christmas celebration. Conversations died away as Opal and Edmund entered, their bedraggled appearance drawing curious stares from the guests. The innkeeper— a substantial man with shrewd eyes and greying hair—looked up from where he was drawing ale behind the bar.

"We're closed to new guests tonight," he said firmly, though not unkindly. "Christmas Day, you understand. Perhaps you could find accommodation at the Crown, two miles down the road."

"We're not seeking accommodation," Opal replied, her voice carrying clearly through the suddenly quiet room. "We're seeking justice for the travellers who have died along these roads—travellers who stopped here before disappearing forever."

The innkeeper's expression sharpened with sudden interest, and several guests shifted uncomfortably at her words. "That's a serious statement, miss. Perhaps you'd better explain yourself."

"My name is Opal Hartwell," she continued, ignoring Edmund's warning touch on her arm. "My father witnessed the murder of Tobias Fletcher three years ago and was framed for theft to silence him. The real killer continues to prey on innocent travellers, and we have evidence that could stop him —if we can find someone brave enough to help us present it to the proper authorities."

A murmur ran through the crowd at her words, and the innkeeper's face grew thoughtful. "Tobias Fletcher," he repeated slowly. "Aye, I remember him. Good man, paid his bills promptly and never caused trouble. Found dead on the London road, they said, killed by bandits."

"Killed by Lord Ashford of Ashford Manor," Edmund said quietly, stepping forward to stand beside Opal. "I'm his son, and I can no longer remain silent about my father's crimes."

The revelation sent a shock through the assembled guests, several of whom began talking in urgent whispers. The innkeeper studied Edmund with new attention, clearly recognizing him despite his dishevelled state.

"Master Edmund," he said carefully. "That's a dangerous accusation to make against your own father."

"I know," Edmund replied. "But it's also true. We have evidence—witness statements, timelines, even the murder weapon. All we need is safe passage to London where officials beyond my father's influence can examine what we've discovered."

The innkeeper was quiet for a long moment, his shrewd eyes moving between Opal and Edmund as he weighed their words against the potential consequences of involvement. Finally, he gestured toward a private parlour off the main taproom.

"Come," he said. "Let's discuss this properly, away from curious ears."

The parlour was small but comfortable, with a cheerful fire burning in the grate and well-worn furniture that spoke of countless private conversations. The innkeeper—who introduced himself as Thomas Whitmore—listened intently as Opal and Edmund presented their evidence, asking pointed questions that demonstrated his familiarity with the victims of the crimes they described.

"This man Fletcher," he said, examining the bloodstained knife with obvious distaste. "I served him myself the night before he died. He was carrying a leather satchel full of gold coins—payment for wool he'd sold in the north country. When they found his body, the satchel was gone."

"Along with any other valuables he might have carried," Opal added. "The same pattern repeated across multiple areas, always with convenient explanations that deflected suspicion from the real perpetrator."

Whitmore set down the knife and leaned back in his chair, his expression troubled. "I've suspected something like this for years," he admitted. "Too many guests disappearing, too many 'accidents' on roads that had been safe for generations. But suspecting and proving are different matters entirely."

"Then you'll help us?" Edmund asked hopefully.

"I'll help you reach London," Whitmore replied carefully. "But I won't lie to you about the dangers you face. Lord Ashford's influence extends far beyond his own county, and there are powerful people who profit from maintaining the current system. Even with evidence as compelling as this, justice is far from guaranteed."

"We understand the risks," Opal said firmly. "But we have to try. Too many innocent people have died already, and my father's memory deserves vindication."

Whitmore nodded slowly, then rose and moved to a writing desk in the corner of the room. "Very well. I have a cousin in London—John Whitmore, a clerk in the Home Office who has access to officials your father can't corrupt. I'll write you a letter of introduction and arrange for one of my drivers to take you there directly."

The relief that flooded through Opal was so intense it left her lightheaded. Finally, after years of suffering and so much desperate planning, they had found someone willing to help them seek justice. It seemed almost too good to be true.

And perhaps, she realized with growing dread, it was.

The sound of horses in the inn's courtyard interrupted her thoughts, followed by authoritative voices demanding accommodation despite the late hour. Through the parlour's window, she could see the glow of multiple lanterns and the shadowy figures of mounted men—too many for ordinary travellers.

"Quickly," Whitmore said, having reached the same conclusion. "There's a back stair that leads to the cellars. You can hide there while I deal with whoever's arrived."

But even as they moved toward the hidden exit, the taproom door burst open with a crash that shook the entire building. Lord Ashford's voice carried clearly through the inn's walls, cold with authority and barely contained rage.

"Whitmore! I know you're here, and I know you're harbouring fugitives. Produce them immediately, or I'll tear this establishment apart board by board."

The innkeeper's face went pale, but his voice remained steady as he called out, "My lord, I'm afraid I don't understand. What fugitives?"

"My son and his accomplice," Lord Ashford snarled. "They murdered two of my men during their escape and stole valuable documents from my estate. I have every right to search these premises. Make your appearance, man!"

It was a lie, of course—they had killed no one during their flight—but it was a clever lie that would justify whatever violence Lord Ashford chose to employ. Worse, it painted them as dangerous criminals rather than seekers of justice, ensuring that anyone who helped them would be seen as aiding murderers.

"The cellar," Whitmore whispered urgently, pushing them toward a narrow door hidden behind a tapestry. "There's a tunnel that connects to the old monastery ruins. If you can reach it without being seen..." And he left them to confront Lord Ashford.

They had no choice but to trust in the innkeeper's knowledge of his own building. The cellar proved to be a maze of storage rooms and wine racks, dimly lit by a few guttering candles. Behind them, they could hear Lord Ashford's men beginning their search of the inn proper, their heavy boots echoing on the wooden floors above.

The tunnel Whitmore had mentioned was cleverly concealed behind a false wall that pivoted on hidden hinges. By sheer luck, Edmund walked directly to it. Beyond lay a narrow passage carved from living rock, clearly ancient and probably dating to the monastery's original construction centuries earlier. They plunged into its depths just as the cellar door crashed open behind them, Lord Ashford's voice echoing down the stone steps.

"Search everything! Every barrel, every corner, every shadow! They're here somewhere, and I want them found!"

The tunnel seemed to stretch forever, its rough walls closing in around them as they stumbled through the darkness. Somewhere behind them, they could hear pursuit—Lord Ashford's men had discovered the hidden entrance and were following them into the depths of the earth. It seemed as if they stumbled on forever as the tunnel continued to open before them.

"There!" a voice shouted from behind them. "Light ahead! They're ahead in the tunnel!"

Edmund grabbed Opal's hand and pulled her forward with desperate urgency, his injured shoulder forgotten in the face of mortal danger. The monastery ruins lay somewhere ahead, offering the promise of multiple escape routes if they could reach them before their pursuers caught up.

They emerged from the tunnel into the ruins of what had once been a great abbey, its broken walls and collapsed roof open to the snowy sky. Christmas night was falling, and in the distance, they could hear the bells of various churches calling worshippers to evening service. The irony was bitter—they were fleeing for their lives on the night Christians celebrated the birth of hope into the world.

"This way," Edmund gasped, leading them toward what remained of the abbey's bell tower. "There's a stair that leads to the upper levels—we might be able to see our pursuers coming and find another way out. Here, rest for a moment. Catch your breath."

Somehow, they managed to evade discovery for a bit of time and were able to take some time to regain their breath. Opal's pounding heart slowed slightly, giving her a small reprieve.

"We must keep going," Edmund finally said. "We'll be trapped otherwise."

As they reached the tower's base, disaster struck. Lord Ashford himself emerged from the tunnel mouth, flanked by armed men whose lanterns cast dancing shadows across the ancient stones. His face was a mask of cold fury, and in his hand, he carried a pistol that glinted dully in the lamplight.

"End of the line," he called, his cultured voice echoing off the ruined walls. "Surrender now, and I might allow you a quick death. Continue running, and I'll ensure you both suffer as traitors deserve."

They were trapped, caught in the open courtyard with nowhere to run and no hope of escape. Lord Ashford's men spread out in a semicircle, cutting off every possible exit while their master advanced with the confident stride of a predator closing in for the kill.

"You've led me quite a chase," Lord Ashford continued, his pale eyes glittering with malicious satisfaction. "But it ends here, tonight, in these holy ruins where so many secrets have been buried over the centuries. How fitting that yours will join them."

Edmund stepped forward, placing himself between Opal and his father's gun. "Let her go," he said quietly. "Your quarrel is with me—she's just a servant who got caught up in family business she doesn't understand."

Lord Ashford's laugh was like breaking glass. "Oh, my dear boy. You really think I don't know exactly what she understands? I've been watching that little wretch for three years, waiting for her to lead me to whatever evidence her thieving father managed to gather. And now, thanks to your romantic foolishness, she's done exactly that."

The revelation hit Opal like a physical blow. Lord Ashford had been using her all along, allowing her to live and suffer at the manor not out of any twisted sense of mercy, but because he knew she would eventually lead him to Samuel's hiding place. Her father's death, their desperate flight, even their current predicament—all of it had been orchestrated by the man who now stood ready to kill them both.

"You monster," she whispered, her voice shaking with rage and grief. "You killed my father twice—once with your lies and once with your patience."

"Your father killed himself the moment he decided to interfere in matters beyond his understanding," Lord Ashford replied coldly. "Just as you're about to kill yourself with your misguided quest for justice."

He raised the pistol, its barrel aimed directly at Opal's heart. Edmund tensed beside her, preparing to throw himself into the line of fire, but they both knew it would be futile. At this range, Lord Ashford could hardly miss, and his men would cut down any survivors before they could take three steps.

The game was over. Lord Ashford had won, just as he had always won, through superior power and absolute ruthlessness. All that remained was to die with dignity and hope that somehow, someday, the truth would come to light despite their failure.

But as Lord Ashford's finger tightened on the trigger, the night exploded with the sound of galloping horses and shouting voices. Mounted figures burst into the ruined courtyard from multiple directions, their uniforms appearing in the lamplight as they surrounded Lord Ashford's men.

"Drop your weapons!" a commanding voice shouted. "By order of His Majesty's magistrates, you are all under arrest!"

The leader of the newcomers was a stern-faced man in official dress who bore the unmistakable authority of high government office. Behind him rode a handful of armed villagers whose weapons were trained on Lord Ashford and his followers with deadly precision.

"Lord Ashford," the official continued, advancing on Lord Ashford with implacable determination. "You are charged with multiple counts of murder, theft, and conspiracy to pervert justice. Surrender your weapon immediately."

Lord Ashford's face had gone white with shock, his pistol wavering as he tried to process this unexpected reversal of fortune. "There must be some mistake," he blustered. "I am Lord Ashford of Ashford Manor, and these are dangerous criminals who—"

"We have Crown witnesses whose testimony will be corroborated by extensive investigation," the official cut him off. "The evidence you thought safely buried will be examined by the highest authorities in the land. Your reign of terror is at an end."

As Lord Ashford's weapon was seized and his hands bound, Opal felt Edmund's arms close around her with desperate relief. Somehow, impossibly, justice had arrived at the very moment when all hope seemed lost.

But how? Who had summoned these officials, and how had they known to find them in the monastery ruins?

The answer came from an unexpected source—Thomas Whitmore, who emerged from behind one of the ruined walls with a grim smile on his weathered face.

"Forgive the deception," he said to Opal and Edmund. "But unbeknownst to anyone I've been working with the authorities for months, gathering evidence of Lord Ashford's crimes. Your arrival tonight provided the final pieces we needed to secure arrest warrants and assemble a proper force to take him into custody."

The innkeeper's true role explained everything—why he had been so quick to help them, why he had known exactly where to send them for safety, why their enemies had seemed to know their every move. He had been playing a far deeper game than either of them had realized, using their desperation to finally spring the trap that would end Lord Ashford's murderous career.

As the Christmas bells continued to ring across the snowy countryside, proclaiming peace on earth and goodwill toward men, Opal allowed herself to believe that miracles were indeed possible. Justice had come at last, carried on the wings of courage and determination and the kind of love that refused to be silenced by any earthly power.

The long nightmare was finally over. And it was only just

beginning to transform into the most beautiful dream either of them had ever dared to imagine.

CHAPTER 10

THE MAGISTRATE'S office in London felt like a sanctuary after the chaos and terror of the past weeks. Opal sat beside Edmund on a hard wooden bench, her hand clasped tightly in his as they waited to give their formal testimony about Lord Ashford's crimes. Through the tall windows, she could see the bustling streets of the capital, where life continued its normal rhythm despite the momentous events that had brought them here.

Three days had passed since that dramatic confrontation in the monastery ruins, three days of careful questioning, document examination, and the gradual unravelling of a conspiracy that had claimed more lives than anyone had initially suspected. The evidence Opal's father had so painstakingly gathered proved to be only the beginning—once investigators began looking seriously at Lord Ashford's activities, the pattern of murder and theft stretched back nearly fifteen years.

"Master Edmund, Miss Hartwell," a clerk appeared at their side, his official bearing softened by genuine sympathy. "Magistrate Thornfield will see you now."

The magistrate's chambers were imposing but not intimidating, lined with law books and dominated by a massive oak desk behind which sat a man whose stern features were tempered by intelligent eyes. Sir Richard Thornfield had been conducting the investigation personally, a mark of how seriously the Crown took charges against a member of the landed gentry.

"Please, be seated," he said, gesturing to chairs positioned before his desk. "I know this has been an ordeal for you both, but I'm pleased to say we're nearing the conclusion of our preliminary investigation."

"What have you discovered?" Edmund asked, his voice carefully controlled. Three days of revelations about his father's crimes had taken their toll, aging him visibly as he struggled to reconcile the man who had raised him with the criminal who stood accused of systematic murder.

"More than we initially hoped, thanks to the evidence your father preserved, Miss Hartwell," Sir Richard replied, shuffling through a thick folder of documents. "Combined with Mr. Whitmore's observations and our own investigations, we've identified at least eleven separate incidents spanning fourteen years. Your father, Lord Ashford, was far more prolific than anyone imagined."

Opal felt Edmund flinch beside her at the words "your father," and she squeezed his hand reassuringly.

"What will happen to him now?" she asked.

"He'll face trial for murder, of course," Sir Richard said gravely. "The evidence is overwhelming, and several witnesses have come forward since his arrest. But there are... complications."

"What sort of complications?" Edmund's voice carried a note of dread.

Sir Richard set down the folder and fixed them both with a serious look. "Lord Ashford's crimes have implicated others—corrupt magistrates who helped cover up investigations, officials who were bribed to look the other way, even members of Parliament who profited from his activities. This case threatens to expose a web of corruption that reaches into the highest levels of government."

"And that's a problem?" Opal asked, confused.

"It's a problem because powerful people are now working very hard to limit the damage," Sir Richard explained. "There's considerable pressure to handle this matter quietly, to avoid a scandal that could shake public confidence in our institutions. Some are suggesting that Lord Ashford might be allowed to plead to lesser charges in exchange for his silence about his co-conspirators."

The implications hit Opal like a physical blow. After everything they had endured, after her father's death and years of turmoil, justice might still be denied in the name of political expediency.

"That's not acceptable," Edmund said firmly, his voice carrying an authority that reminded Opal he was still, despite everything, the son of a lord. "My father is a murderer who has evaded justice for years. He must face the full consequences of his crimes, regardless of who else might be embarrassed by the revelations."

"I agree completely," Sir Richard said with evident relief. "But I needed to gauge your commitment before proceeding. The path ahead will not be easy—you'll both face intense scrutiny, possible threats from those who wish this matter buried, and certainly social ostracism from certain quarters of society."

"We understand," Opal replied. "But my father died believing that truth would eventually prevail. I won't dishonour his memory by accepting anything less than complete justice. And besides, I have lived with social ostracism my entire life."

Sir Richard nodded. "Very well. Then I have a proposal that might serve all our interests. The Crown is prepared to offer you both protection and compensation in exchange for your cooperation in a broader investigation. We want to expose not just Lord Ashford's crimes, but the entire network of corruption that enabled them."

"What sort of protection?" Edmund asked practically.

"New identities, if necessary. Relocation to secure accommodations. Financial support to ensure you can rebuild your lives away from those who might wish you harm." Sir Richard paused meaningfully. "The Crown recognizes that you've both sacrificed a great deal in the service of justice. It's only fitting that you be rewarded for your courage."

The offer was generous beyond anything Opal had dared hope for, but it came with its own complications. New identities meant abandoning everything that connected them to their past—Edmund's family name, her father's memory, the very foundations of who they were.

"We need time to consider," Edmund said after a long pause. "This decision will affect the rest of our lives."

"Of course," Sir Richard agreed. "But don't take too long. Lord Ashford's allies are already working to undermine the case against him. The longer we delay, the more opportunity they have to destroy evidence or intimidate witnesses."

As they left the magistrate's office and stepped into the grey December afternoon, Opal felt the weight of decision pressing upon her shoulders. Around them, London continued its bustling activity—merchants hawking their wares, carriages clattering over cobblestones, the general chaos of a great city in the final days before the new year.

"What are you thinking?" Edmund asked as they walked slowly through the crowded streets.

"I'm thinking about my father," Opal replied honestly. "He spent three years gathering evidence, sacrificing his health and ultimately his life to ensure justice could be done. How can I accept anything less than a full accounting of Lord Ashford's crimes?"

"Even if it means spending the rest of our lives looking over our shoulders?" Edmund's question was gentle but pointed. "Even if it means we can never live openly as the people we truly are?"

Opal considered this carefully. The prospect of a new life, free from the shadows of the past, was undeniably appealing. But it would also mean that Samuel Hartwell's name would never be truly cleared, that he would remain remembered as a thief rather than the honest man he had been.

"There might be another way," she said slowly, an idea beginning to form in her mind. "What if we could expose your father's crimes without destroying our own futures? What if we could find a way to have both justice and the life we want together?"

Edmund stopped walking and turned to face her fully. "What are you suggesting?"

"I'm suggesting we think carefully, the way your father did for all those years," Opal replied, her excitement growing as the plan took shape in her mind. "He succeeded for so long because he was smarter than his enemies, because he anticipated their moves and stayed one step ahead. What if we did the same thing, but in service of justice instead of crime?"

They found a quiet pub where they could discuss Opal's emerging plan without being overheard. Over steaming cups and the gentle murmur of conversation from other patrons, she outlined her idea with growing confidence.

"Your father's greatest weakness has always been his arrogance," she began. "He believes himself untouchable because of his position and connections. But what if we could use that arrogance against him?"

"How?" Edmund asked, leaning forward with interest.

"By giving him exactly what he expects—a quiet resolution that protects his powerful friends while seemingly letting him escape the worst consequences of his crimes," Opal explained. "But we make sure the truth comes out in a way that can't be suppressed or ignored."

Edmund's eyes began to gleam with understanding. "You want to set a trap."

"I want to let him think he's won, right up until the moment he realizes he's lost everything," Opal corrected. "Remember, I've spent three years watching how your family operates, learning their weaknesses and blind spots. I know how to play the role they expect from me."

The plan that emerged over the next hour was audacious in its simplicity. They would appear to accept a compromise solution—Lord Ashford pleading guilty to manslaughter rather than murder, accepting exile rather than execution, his co-conspirators remaining unnamed in exchange for his cooperation. But behind the scenes, they would be working with Sir Richard and other reformers to ensure the full truth emerged in ways that couldn't be suppressed.

"It's dangerous," Edmund warned as they prepared to leave the pub. "If my father suspects we're playing a double game, he'll have us killed regardless of any protection the Crown might offer."

"Everything we've done has been dangerous," Opal replied. "But this time we'll have the advantage of playing by our own rules instead of reacting to his moves."

When they returned to Sir Richard's office that evening, they found the magistrate in conference with a distinguished gentleman whose expensive clothes and confident bearing marked him as a person of considerable importance. He was introduced as Lord Chancellor Westbrook, one of the most powerful legal officials in the kingdom.

"Ah, Miss Hartwell, Master Edmund," Sir Richard said as they entered. "Perfect timing. Lord Westbrook has some interesting news about your case."

The Lord Chancellor's smile was pleasant but calculating as he studied them both with obvious interest. "Indeed. It seems certain parties have been in contact with my office, expressing concern about the... scope... of our investigation into Lord Ashford's activities."

"What sort of concern?" Edmund asked warily.

"The sort that comes with substantial offers of compensation for discretion," Lord Westbrook replied bluntly. "It appears your father's crimes have implicated more people than we initially realized, Master Edmund. People with the resources and motivation to ensure this matter is resolved quietly."

Opal felt her heart sink. Despite all their efforts, despite the evidence and witnesses they had gathered, political pressure was mounting to protect the guilty at the expense of justice.

"However," Lord Westbrook continued, his tone shifting subtly, "I find myself philosophically opposed to such compromises. Justice delayed is justice denied, as the saying goes. Which is why I'm prepared to offer you both my full support in pursuing this matter to its logical conclusion."

"What does that mean, practically speaking?" Edmund asked.

"It means we proceed with full prosecutions for everyone involved, regardless of their position or connections," Lord Westbrook replied firmly. "It means your father faces trial for murder, his co-conspirators face charges for their roles in covering up his crimes, and the entire corrupt network is exposed to public scrutiny."

"And the consequences for us?" Opal asked.

"Significant, I won't lie to you," the Lord Chancellor admitted. "You'll both need to testify publicly, which will make you targets for retaliation. You'll face social ostracism. And you'll need to be prepared for a lifetime of vigilance against those who blame you for their downfall."

It was exactly what they had expected, but hearing it stated so bluntly still sent a chill through Opal's heart. She thought of her father, who had faced similar choices and ultimately sacrificed everything in the pursuit of truth.

"But," Lord Westbrook continued, "you'll also have the satisfaction of knowing that justice has been served, that future victims have been protected, and that your courage has helped reform a system that has failed too many innocent people."

Edmund reached for Opal's hand, his fingers warm and steady against her palm. "We'll do it," he said without hesitation. "Whatever the personal cost, we'll see this through to the end."

"Are you certain?" Sir Richard asked, his concern evident. "Once we begin public proceedings, there will be no going back. Your lives will never be the same."

Opal thought of her father's dying words, his plea for her not to let hatred consume her, his faith that good people still existed in the world who would stand up for what was right. She thought of the travellers who had died on dark roads, their murders covered up by corruption and indifference. She thought of the life she and Edmund might build together, founded on truth rather than compromise.

"I'm certain," she said firmly. "My father died believing that justice was worth any sacrifice. I won't prove him wrong by choosing comfort over truth."

Lord Westbrook nodded approvingly. "Very well. Then we proceed. Lord Ashford's trial will begin in the new year, and you'll both be called as key witnesses. I warn you—his defense will attempt to destroy your credibility by any means necessary. They'll attack your character, your motives, your relationship with each other. It will be brutal."

"We'll face it together," Edmund said, squeezing Opal's hand. "Whatever they throw at us, we'll stand firm in the truth."

As they left the government buildings and stepped into the London twilight, Opal felt a complex mixture of fear and anticipation. The road ahead would be difficult, fraught with dangers they could barely imagine. But it was their road, chosen freely in service of justice, and they would walk it together.

"Do you regret it?" Edmund asked as they made their way

through the gaslit streets toward their modest lodgings. "Choosing this path instead of accepting a quiet resolution?"

"Never," Opal replied without hesitation. "My father spent three years in hiding so that this moment might come. How could I honour his memory by settling for anything less than complete vindication?"

"Even if it means we'll always be looking over our shoulders? Even if it means our children will grow up knowing their grandfather was a murderer?"

Opal stopped walking and turned to face him fully, her heart racing at the implications of his words. "Our children?"

Edmund's face flushed red in the gaslight. "I... that is... I hope... if you would consider..." He took a deep breath and started again. "Opal, I love you. I want to marry you, to build a life together regardless of what society thinks about our different stations. But I should have asked you about your feelings before presuming to speak of such things."

The proposal was hardly romantic—standing on a busy London street with the sounds of traffic and commerce all around them—but it was perfectly them. Two people who had found love amid darkness, who had chosen truth over comfort, justice over safety.

"Yes," she said simply, reaching up to touch his face with gentle fingers. "Yes to marriage, yes to children, yes to a life built on honesty instead of lies. Yes to everything, as long as we face it together."

When he kissed her there on the crowded street, Opal didn't care who might be watching or what scandalous gossip their public display might generate. She had spent too many years hiding her feelings, suppressing her hopes, accepting less than she deserved simply because the world told her she should.

No more. The truth had set them free in more ways than one, and she intended to live that freedom fully, regardless of the consequences.

⚜

AS THE NEW year approached and Lord Ashford's trial loomed ahead, Opal allowed herself to dream of the future she and Edmund would build together. It wouldn't be easy—nothing worthwhile ever was—but it would be theirs, earned through courage and sacrifice and an unshakeable commitment to doing what was right.

Her father's memory would be honoured. Justice would be served. And love, despite all the forces arrayed against it, would triumph in the end.

The long nightmare was finally ending. And the most beautiful dream of all was just beginning.

CHAPTER 11

THE OLD BAILEY courthouse stood like a fortress of justice in the heart of London, its imposing stone facade weathered by centuries of legal proceedings that had shaped the very fabric of English law. On this bitter January morning, crowds had gathered despite the bone-chilling wind, drawn by the promise of witnessing the most sensational trial in recent memory—the prosecution of Lord James Ashford for multiple counts of murder.

Opal pulled her modest cloak tighter as she and Edmund made their way through the throng of spectators, journalists, and curiosity seekers who pressed against the courthouse steps. Three weeks had passed since their fateful decision to pursue full justice, and in that time the case had captured the public imagination in ways none of them had anticipated. Broadsheets trumpeted headlines about "The Murdering

Lord" and "Love Conquers All," while society gossips whispered scandalous tales about the aristocrat's son who had betrayed his own father for a servant girl.

"Stay close," Edmund murmured, his arm protective on her shoulder as they navigated the crowd. "Some of these people aren't here out of support for justice."

Indeed, Opal could see hostile faces among the spectators—well-dressed men and women whose expressions suggested they viewed her as a dangerous revolutionary who threatened the natural order of society. The past three weeks had brought a steady stream of anonymous threats, nasty letters, and social snubs that made their position abundantly clear: in the eyes of many, she was an upstart servant who had seduced her better into betraying his own class.

Inside the courthouse, the atmosphere was charged with tension and expectation. The gallery was packed with observers representing every level of society, from titled lords and ladies who had come to witness their peer's downfall to working people who saw in this trial a rare opportunity for the powerful to face consequences for their crimes. At the centre of it all sat Lord Ashford himself, his bearing still proud despite the shackles on his wrists, his pale eyes scanning the courtroom with the calculating gaze of a predator even in captivity.

"Members of the jury," the prosecutor began, his voice carrying clearly through the hushed courtroom, "you are about to hear evidence of crimes so heinous, so systematically evil, that they challenge our very conception of what it means to be human. The defendant, Lord James Ashford, stands accused not merely of murder, but of a campaign of terror that has claimed at least eleven innocent lives over the course of fourteen years."

Opal felt Edmund tense beside her as the prosecutor outlined the case against his father in devastating detail. Each victim was named, their stories told with compassionate precision that brought tears to many eyes in the gallery. The merchant traveling home to his family for Christmas. The young couple journeying to their wedding. The elderly widow carrying her life savings to her daughter's home. All dead by Lord Ashford's hand, their murders disguised as random acts of banditry while their killer lived in luxury on the proceeds of their stolen wealth.

"The Crown will prove," the prosecutor continued, "that Lord Ashford's crimes were enabled by a network of corrupt officials who turned blind eyes to mounting evidence in exchange for generous bribes. We will show that when honest men like Samuel Hartwell threatened to expose these crimes, they were silenced through false accusations and systematic persecution. And we will demonstrate that this conspiracy of evil was finally brought to light through the extraordinary courage of two young people who risked everything in the pursuit of justice."

When Opal was called to testify, the walk to the witness box felt like the longest journey of her life. Every eye in the packed courtroom was upon her, and she could feel the weight of history in this moment. Her testimony would either vindicate her father's memory and bring justice to Lord Ashford's victims, or it would be dismissed as the fantasy of a hysterical servant girl with delusions of grandeur.

"State your name for the record," the prosecutor began gently.

"Opal Hartwell," she replied, her voice clear and steady despite the uproar in her stomach. "Daughter of Samuel Hartwell, blacksmith's assistant of Ashford village."

"Miss Hartwell, I want you to think back to the night of November twenty-second, three years ago. Can you tell the jury what happened in your cottage that evening?"

Opal took a deep breath and began the story she had rehearsed countless times in her mind—her father's terrified arrival, his desperate warnings about Lord Ashford's crimes, the discovery of planted evidence that would frame him as a thief. She spoke clearly and without embellishment, letting the simple truth of her words carry their own weight.

But it was when she described finding her father in his hidden chamber, dying of consumption after three years of exile, that the true emotional impact of Lord Ashford's crimes became clear to everyone in the courtroom.

"He could barely speak by then," Opal said, tears flowing freely down her cheeks as she relived that terrible moment. "But he used his last breath to make me promise that I would clear his name, that I would see justice done for all the innocent people who had died. He died believing that good people still existed who would stand up for what was right."

"And did your father give you any evidence to support his claims about Lord Ashford's crimes?"

"Yes," Opal replied, gesturing toward the collection of documents that lay on the evidence table. "He had spent three years gathering witness statements, documenting the pattern of murders, even retrieving the actual weapon used in the killings. He knew he was dying, so he made sure the truth would survive even if he didn't."

The defense attorney's cross-examination was every bit as brutal as Lord Westbrook had warned it would be. He attacked Opal's character, her motives, her relationship with Edmund, suggesting that she was a scheming servant who had seduced her master into helping her concoct an elaborate revenge fantasy against his family.

"Isn't it true, Miss Hartwell, that you harboured resentment against Lord Ashford's family for your reduced circumstances?" the defense attorney pressed. "Isn't it possible that your father filled your head with lies about his innocence, and you've constructed this entire conspiracy to justify your own desires for revenge and social advancement?"

"No, sir," Opal replied firmly. "My father was the most honest man I ever knew. He taught me that truth was more important than comfort, that justice was worth any sacrifice. Everything he told me has been proven correct by the evidence we've presented."

"But you admit you've been romantically involved with the defendant's son? That you stand to gain considerably from Lord Ashford's conviction?"

The implication was clear—that she was nothing more than a gold-digging servant who had manipulated Edmund into betraying his own family. Opal felt anger rise in her chest, but she forced herself to remain calm and dignified.

"I love Edmund Ashford," she said clearly, looking directly at the jury. "But I also love justice. If I had wanted comfort and security, I would have kept silent about what I knew. Instead, I chose to risk everything—my life, my future, my happiness —because I couldn't let my father's death be meaningless."

When Edmund took the stand, the impact was even more dramatic. Here was the defendant's own son, heir to his title and fortune, testifying against his own father with unwavering conviction. The defense attorney tried to paint him as a young man corrupted by infatuation, but Edmund's calm dignity and obvious sincerity made such attacks ring hollow.

"I have lived my entire life benefiting from wealth built on crime," Edmund testified. "Every comfort I enjoyed, every privilege I took for granted, was paid for with innocent blood.

I cannot undo the past, but I can ensure that no more innocents die while I remain silent."

"And you're willing to destroy your own family's reputation for this servant girl?" the defense attorney asked sneeringly.

"I'm willing to do what's right," Edmund replied without hesitation. "My father destroyed our family's reputation the moment he chose crime. I'm simply ensuring that his crimes finally face consequences."

The prosecution's case was methodical and devastating. Witness after witness took the stand to describe Lord Ashford's suspicious behaviour, the pattern of deaths that followed his travels, the corruption that had protected him for so long. The evidence was overwhelming—documents, weapons, testimonies that painted a picture of systematic evil that shocked even the most cynical observers.

But it was the testimony of Thomas Whitmore, the innkeeper who had helped expose the conspiracy, that proved most damaging to Lord Ashford's defense.

"I've been watching wealthy travellers disappear for fifteen years," Whitmore said grimly. "Good, honest people who stopped at my inn and were found dead on the roads the next morning. I suspected Lord Ashford early on, but what could an innkeeper do against such powerful enemies? It wasn't until Miss Hartwell and Master Edmund provided the missing evidence that I finally had the proof needed to act."

"Why didn't you come forward sooner?" the prosecutor asked.

"Because I was afraid," Whitmore admitted honestly. "I knew what happened to people who crossed Lord Ashford—they ended up dead or framed for crimes they didn't commit. I wanted to see justice done, but I also wanted to live long enough to see it happen."

The defence's case rested largely on character assassination and appeals to class prejudice. Lord Ashford's attorney painted him as a respected member of the nobility who was being destroyed by the lies of vengeful servants and misguided reformers. They brought witnesses to testify to his charitable works, his standing in the community, his reputation as a gentleman of honour and distinction.

But when Lord Ashford himself took the stand in his own defense, his arrogance proved to be his undoing. Rather than showing remorse or even attempting to explain his actions, he maintained his innocence with such cold disdain for his accusers that even his supporters began to doubt his credibility.

"The testimony you've heard is nothing but the fantasy of hysterical servants and corrupt officials seeking to destroy a better man than themselves," he declared, his pale eyes sweeping the courtroom with obvious contempt. "I am a lord of this realm, descended from men who built this nation's greatness. I will not be brought low by the lies of those who seek to tear down everything noble and worthy in our society."

The prosecutor's cross-examination of Lord Ashford was a masterpiece of legal strategy. Rather than attacking him directly, he simply let the man's own words condemn him, drawing out his arrogance and contempt until even the most class-conscious observers could see the monster beneath the aristocratic facade.

"You maintain your innocence despite overwhelming evidence to the contrary," the prosecutor observed. "Do you expect this jury to believe that eleven separate investigations were all wrong? That dozens of witnesses have conspired to lie about your activities?"

"I expect this jury to remember their place," Lord Ashford replied coldly. "I expect them to understand the difference between the word of a peer and the gossip of servants and innkeepers."

It was exactly the wrong thing to say. The jury, composed largely of merchants and tradesmen, bristled visibly at the implication that their judgment was somehow inferior to aristocratic privilege. Whatever sympathy they might have felt for a fellow member of the upper classes evaporated in the face of such naked contempt.

The final arguments lasted two days, with both sides marshalling every resource at their disposal. The defense made passionate appeals to tradition, order, and the danger of allowing servants to destroy their betters through false accusations. The prosecution focused relentlessly on the evidence, the victims, and the simple moral truth that murder was wrong regardless of who committed it.

When the jury retired to deliberate, Opal and Edmund found themselves in the peculiar position of waiting to learn whether justice would be served or whether wealth and privilege would once again triumph over truth. They sat together in a small anteroom, holding hands and trying not to think about what would happen if the verdict went against them.

"Whatever happens," Edmund said quietly, "I want you to know that I have no regrets. Standing up for what's right was worth any price."

"Even if it means losing everything?" Opal asked, voicing the fear that had haunted them both throughout the trial.

"Especially then," Edmund replied firmly. "What good is wealth built on innocent blood? What value is a title earned through wrong-doing? I'd rather be a poor man with a clear conscience than a rich one with blood on his hands."

The jury deliberated for six hours—an eternity for those waiting to learn their fate. When they finally returned to the courtroom, their faces revealed nothing of their decision. The foreman stood, a middle-aged tradesman whose weathered hands spoke of honest labour and faced the judge with obvious gravity.

"Have you reached a verdict?" the judge asked.

"We have, Your Honour."

"On the charge of murder in the first degree, how do you find?"

The pause seemed to last forever, though it was probably only seconds. In that suspended moment, Opal could hear her heart beating, could feel Edmund's hand tightening around hers, could sense the held breath of hundreds of observers waiting to learn whether justice would prevail.

"Guilty, Your Honour."

The word seemed to echo through the courthouse like thunder, followed by an explosion of voices as the crowd reacted to the verdict. Some cheered, others wept, still others sat in stunned silence as the implications sank in. For the first time in living memory, one of England's lords had been held accountable for crimes against common people.

But the celebration was premature. As the judge prepared to pronounce sentence, a commotion at the back of the courtroom drew everyone's attention. A group of well-dressed men were forcing their way through the crowd, their official bearing and obvious authority creating a path through the packed gallery.

"Your Honour," one of them called out, "I must request an immediate recess. New evidence has come to light that bears on this case."

The judge's expression grew troubled as he recognized the speaker—Sir Reginald Blackwood, one of the most powerful men in the Home Office and a figure whose influence reached into the highest levels of government. His presence here, at this moment, could only mean one thing: the forces Lord Westbrook had warned them about were making their move.

"What sort of evidence?" the judge asked warily.

"Evidence that calls into question the credibility of the Crown's key witnesses," Sir Reginald replied smoothly. "Evidence that suggests this entire prosecution has been based on fabricated testimony and forged documents."

Opal felt the blood drain from her face as she realized what was happening. Despite their victory, despite the jury's verdict, the corrupt network that had protected Lord Ashford for so long was attempting one final desperate gambit to save their co-conspirator. If they succeeded, not only would justice be denied, but she and Edmund would likely face charges of perjury and conspiracy themselves.

The game was far from over. If anything, the most dangerous moves were yet to come.

But as she looked around the courtroom—at the faces of ordinary people who had come to witness justice being done, at the journalists whose reports would carry this story across the nation, at Edmund whose love and courage had made this moment possible—Opal felt a quiet confidence that truth would ultimately prevail.

Her father had died believing that good people still existed who would stand up for what was right. The jury's verdict proved he had been correct. The price of justice was high, but some things were worth any sacrifice. And sometimes, even against impossible odds, truth really was stronger than all the lies that sought to suppress it.

CHAPTER 12

THE COURTROOM FELL into an expectant hush as Sir Reginald Blackwood's dramatic intervention threatened to overturn everything they had fought to achieve. Opal felt Edmund's hand tighten around hers as the full implications of this moment became clear—they were witnessing the final, desperate gambit of the corrupt network that had protected Lord Ashford for so long.

"Your Honour," Sir Reginald continued, his voice carrying the smooth authority of a man accustomed to having his words treated as commands, "I submit that this court has been deliberately misled by witnesses whose testimony cannot be trusted. The Crown's case rests entirely on evidence provided by individuals with clear motives for revenge and personal gain."

Judge Harrison's weathered face showed deep scepticism as he examined the documents Sir Reginald had produced. "These are serious allegations, Sir Reginald. Are you suggesting that my court has been the victim of an elaborate deception?"

"I'm suggesting that romantic infatuation and class resentment have created a conspiracy against an innocent man," Sir Reginald replied smoothly. "The so-called evidence against Lord Ashford was fabricated by Samuel Hartwell during his three years as a fugitive, with the assistance of accomplices who shared his desire for revenge against their social betters."

The accusation hung in the air like poison, threatening to corrupt everything they had achieved. Opal could see doubt flickering in some jurors' eyes, could hear whispers spreading through the gallery as society's most influential voices began to reassert their power over the proceedings.

But before Judge Harrison could respond to Sir Reginald's challenge, another voice cut through the tension—clear, authoritative, and completely unexpected.

"Your Honour, if I may?"

Every head in the courtroom turned toward the speaker, and Opal's heart leaped with sudden hope as she recognized the distinctive figure of Lord Chancellor Westbrook himself, rising from a seat in the gallery's front row. His presence here was unprecedented—the highest legal officer in the kingdom did not typically attend criminal trials unless matters of supreme importance were at stake.

"Lord Chancellor," Judge Harrison said, clearly startled by this development. "I... of course, Your Lordship. How may the court assist you?"

Lord Westbrook moved with deliberate dignity to the centre of the courtroom, his every gesture commanding absolute attention from the packed gallery. When he spoke, his voice carried the weight of ultimate legal authority.

"Your Honour, I appear here today not in any official capacity, but as a concerned citizen who has watched this trial with great interest," he began, his piercing gaze sweeping across the assembled crowd. "I have observed the evidence presented, listened to the testimony given, and witnessed the jury's careful deliberation. In my considered opinion, justice has been served in accordance with the highest traditions of English law."

Sir Reginald's face had gone pale at this unexpected intervention. "Lord Chancellor, surely you cannot support the conviction of a peer based on the word of servants and innkeepers?"

"I support the conviction of a murderer based on overwhelming evidence of his crimes," Lord Westbrook replied with steel in his voice. "The notion that a man's birth entitles him to commit murder with impunity is precisely the sort of corruption that brings disgrace upon our entire system of justice."

The Lord Chancellor turned to address the court directly, his words carrying across the hushed courtroom like a clarion call for righteousness.

"Members of the jury, your verdict stands as a beacon of hope for all who believe that justice should be blind to wealth and privilege. You have proven that in England, no man—regardless of his title or connections—is above the law. History will remember this moment as a triumph of truth over corruption, of courage over fear."

But Lord Westbrook was not finished. As Sir Reginald sputtered protests about proper procedure and jurisdictional authority, the Lord Chancellor produced a sealed document from within his robes.

"Furthermore," he continued, "I bear a message from His Majesty himself, who has followed this case with considerable interest. The Crown recognizes that the corruption exposed in this trial extends far beyond the crimes of one man, however heinous those crimes may be. Therefore, His Majesty has authorized a full investigation into all officials who may have enabled Lord Ashford's activities through bribery, intimidation, or wilful blindness."

The implications of this announcement sent shockwaves through the courtroom. Sir Reginald and his companions suddenly found themselves not as saviours of the established order, but as potential targets of royal investigation. Their confident expressions crumbled as they realized that their attempt to rescue Lord Ashford had instead exposed them to official scrutiny.

"The Crown further directs," Lord Westbrook continued inexorably, "that all persons who have courageously come forward to expose these crimes be granted full protection and compensation for their service to justice. Miss Hartwell and Master Edmund, your sacrifice in the pursuit of truth exemplifies the highest virtues of British citizenship."

As the Lord Chancellor's words echoed through the courtroom, Opal felt a wave of relief so intense it left her lightheaded. Not only had justice been preserved, but the very highest authorities in the land had explicitly endorsed their actions. The years of suffering, the moments of terror, the constant fear of retaliation—all of it had been vindicated by this moment of official recognition.

Judge Harrison, clearly overwhelmed by these unprecedented developments, called for a brief recess to consider the new circumstances. But when court reconvened thirty minutes later, his course was clear.

"Lord James Ashford," he said, his voice carrying the weight of final judgment, "you have been found guilty by a jury of your peers of multiple counts of murder in the first degree. The evidence against you has been overwhelming, and your contempt for this court and the principles of justice it represents has been evident throughout these proceedings."

Lord Ashford stood to receive his sentence with the same cold arrogance he had displayed throughout the trial, but Opal could see cracks in his facade now—a tremor in his hands, a tightness around his eyes that spoke of a man finally confronting the consequences of his actions.

"It is the judgment of this court," Judge Harrison continued, "that you shall be hanged by the neck until dead. Said execution to take place at dawn on the fifteenth day of February, in the year of our Lord eighteen hundred and forty-five. May God have mercy on your soul, for this court has none to offer."

The sentence fell like a thunderclap, followed by an eruption of voices from the gallery. Some cheered the prospect of final justice, others wept with relief, while still others sat in stunned silence at witnessing the fall of one who had seemed untouchable just hours before.

Lord Ashford himself showed no emotion as the sentence was pronounced, but as the guards moved to escort him from the courtroom, his pale eyes found Opal's across the crowded space. For a moment, she saw not the cold killer who had destroyed so many lives, but simply a broken man facing the ultimate consequence of his choices. There was no remorse in his gaze, only a kind of bitter acknowledgment that the game was finally over.

As the courtroom slowly emptied and the immediate drama faded, Opal and Edmund found themselves surrounded by well-wishers, journalists, and curious observers who wanted to congratulate them on their victory. But all she could think about was her father—Samuel Hartwell, who had died believing that justice was possible if good people had the courage to fight for it.

"He would be so proud," Edmund whispered in her ear as they made their way through the crowd. "Your father's faith in justice has been completely vindicated."

"But your mother?" Opal asked quietly, suddenly hurting for the woman.

"My mother..." Edmund sighed, and a deep sadness was etched on his face. "I will go to her and explain, but I am certain she will already have heard all the news." He sighed again. "Of course, she would never have stepped into the courthouse, and I don't fault her for that. I just wish—I just wish with all my heart I wish it hadn't happened. None of it. My father..." His voice broke and Opal knew she was hurting for him, hurting for what might have been.

"I'm so sorry this has destroyed your family," Opal whispered.

"I am sorry, too," he said. Then he straightened his shoulders as if bracing himself to carry on, despite the ruin his father had made.

"You will see him before he's hanged?"

"He will not want to see me." His eyes welled with tears. "He will ... hate me. I... I..." He stopped and drew in a shuddering breath. "It had to be done. But I am so deeply sorry..."

Opal took his hand in hers, hurting for this brave man who had done the unthinkable. Together, they walked through the courthouse doors.

Outside the courthouse, London was celebrating. News of the verdict had spread quickly through the city's streets, and crowds had gathered to cheer the two young people who had brought down one of the kingdom's most powerful killers. Merchants offered them free meals, working men tipped their caps in respect, and even some members of the gentry nodded approvingly as they passed.

Edmund kept a stoic face through it all, but it was clear he was hurting deeply.

And then, they were approached by an elderly woman whose worn clothes and callused hands marked her as someone who had known hard labour and harder times.

"Miss," she said, her voice trembling with emotion, "I wanted to thank you and him. My brother Tom was killed on the London road five years ago—beaten and robbed, they said. The constables said it was bandits and closed the case without investigation. Now I know who really killed him. My brother can rest in peace now, and so can I."

The woman pressed a small token into Opal's hand—a simple wooden cross that had clearly been carved with loving care.

"This was Tom's," she explained. "He always said it would protect him from evil. Didn't work for him, but maybe it will for you."

As the woman disappeared back into the crowd, Opal clutched the cross tightly, feeling the weight of all the lives that had been lost to Lord Ashford's greed. Justice had been served, but it could not bring back the dead or undo the suffering their families had endured. All she and Edmund could do was ensure that their sacrifice had meaning, that the future would be different because of what had been revealed in that courtroom.

⟡

THREE WEEKS LATER, on a crisp February morning with spring beginning to stir in London's parks and gardens, Opal stood before the altar of St. Andrew's Church in her wedding dress. The gown was simple but beautiful, its ivory silk and delicate lace signifying an earlier time when love had triumphed over hardship in the Hartwell family.

Edmund waited for her at the altar, resplendent in his finest clothes but bearing little resemblance to the privileged young lord he had been just months before. The trials had changed him, stripping away his aristocratic assumptions, replacing them with a deeper understanding of justice, sacrifice, and the true value of human dignity. He was no longer Master Edmund Ashford, heir to a corrupt fortune—he was simply

Edmund, a man who had chosen love over privilege and truth over comfort.

The wedding ceremony was attended by an unusual mixture of guests. Lord Chancellor Westbrook served as one witness, his presence lending official dignity to the proceedings. Thomas Whitmore had travelled from his inn to stand with them, representing all those who had risked their own safety to expose the truth. Sir Richard Thornfield was there, along with several other officials who had supported their cause despite considerable pressure to remain silent.

But perhaps most importantly, the church was filled with ordinary people—servants and workers, merchants and crafts-men, all those who had found hope in the story of two young people who had refused to accept injustice simply because it came from those in power.

The most notable absence of course, Edmund's parents.

As Opal walked down the aisle toward her future, she carried with her the wooden cross the elderly woman had given her, along with the iron key her father had pressed into her palm during their last moments together. Both were symbols of faith—faith in justice, faith in love, faith in the possibility that good could triumph over evil if people had the courage to fight for what was right.

"Dearly beloved," the minister began, his voice carrying clearly through the packed church, "we are gathered here today to witness the union of two souls who have proven that love is stronger than any earthly power, that truth is more precious than any worldly treasure, and that justice is worth any sacrifice."

When they spoke their vows, promising to love and honour each other for the rest of their lives, Opal felt her father's presence as strongly as if he were standing beside her. Samuel Hartwell had died believing that his daughter would find happiness and justice in equal measure. Today, both of those prayers were being answered.

The wedding breakfast was held at the Golden Lamb, where Thomas Whitmore had insisted on providing the finest feast his establishment could offer. As the guests raised their glasses in celebration, Lord Chancellor Westbrook stood to offer a toast that would long be remembered by all who heard it.

"To Edmund and Opal," he said, his voice carrying the weight of official authority but warmed by genuine affection, "who have proven that the greatest nobility lies not in blood or birth, but in courage and character. Your love story will be told for generations as proof that justice and happiness can triumph over even the most powerful forces of corruption and greed."

As the celebration continued around them, Opal and Edmund found a quiet moment together in the inn's garden, where early spring flowers were beginning to bloom despite the lingering winter cold.

"Do you wonder what your father would think of all this?" Opal asked, her hand resting in Edmund's as they watched the sunset paint the sky in shades of gold and rose.

"I know exactly what he would think," Edmund replied with quiet conviction. "He would be horrified by the exposure of his crimes, furious about the loss of his wealth and position, and completely unrepentant about the lives he destroyed. But I cannot ... I cannot care what he thinks. The only father's opinion that matters to me now is your father's."

"Mine?" Opal looked at him in confusion.

"Samuel Hartwell's," Edmund clarified, his voice soft with emotion. "He was the kind of man I hope to become—honest, brave, willing to sacrifice everything for what's right. If I could earn even a fraction of his respect, I'll consider my life well-lived."

As they stood together in the gathering twilight, surrounded by the first flowers of spring and sustained by a love that had been tested in the fires of adversity, Opal felt a deep sense of completion. The journey that had begun with her father's terrified flight into the night had ended with justice served and love triumphant.

But more than that, it had ended with the knowledge that they had helped change the world for the better. Lord Ashford's execution had sent a clear message that even the most powerful could not escape justice forever. The investigation Lord Westbrook had promised was already uncovering other cases of corruption and abuse, slowly but steadily reforming a system that had failed too many innocent people.

"What shall we do now?" Edmund asked as they prepared to return to their guests. "Where shall we make our home?"

Opal smiled, thinking of all the possibilities that lay before them. They had enough money—compensation from the Crown, along with part of Edmund's small allowance he had managed to save in the past—to live wherever they chose. They could remain in London, move to the countryside, even travel abroad if they wished.

"Somewhere we can help others," she said finally. "Somewhere we can use what we've learned to make sure that justice isn't just a privilege of the wealthy. My father spent his life believing that good people could change the world if they had the courage to try. I want to prove him right."

Edmund's smile was radiant as he pulled her closer. "Then that's what we'll do. Together, we'll help build a world where birth and wealth matter less than character and courage. Where servant girls can marry nobleman's sons and live happily ever after, because love really can conquer all."

As they walked back toward the warmth and laughter of their wedding celebration, Opal touched the cross and key she wore around her neck—symbols of faith and secrets, of sacrifice and salvation. Her father's memory would live on through their work, his faith in justice vindicated by their courage, his love for his daughter fulfilled in the happiness she had found with the man who had chosen truth over privilege.

As Opal and Edmund stepped back into the light and warmth of their wedding feast, they carried with them the absolute certainty that some things—love, truth, justice—really were stronger than any earthly power that tried to stand against them.

The future stretched before them like an unwritten book, its pages blank and ready to be filled with new stories of hope, courage, and the endless possibility that came from choosing what was right over what was easy. And they would write those stories together, hand in hand, heart to heart, sustained by a love that had been tested in the darkest hours and emerged stronger than ever.

The blacksmith's daughter had become something more than she had ever dared dream, not through luck or privilege, but through courage, love, and an unshakeable faith in the power of truth. And that, perhaps, was the most important lesson of all.

EPILOGUE

The cottage stood at the edge of Millbrook village like a perfect illustration from a children's storybook, its thatched roof dusted with fresh snow and warm golden light spilling from every mullioned window into the crisp December night. Smoke curled lazily from the chimney, carrying with it the mingled scents of roasting goose, Christmas pudding, and the pine boughs that decorated every room within.

Opal Ashford—she still marvelled at the name sometimes— stood at the kitchen window, her hands resting on the gentle swell of her belly where their second child grew steadily toward a spring birth. Through the glass, she could see Edmund in the front garden, helping their three-year-old son Thomas build a snowman with the serious concentration that both father and son brought to any project they undertook together.

"Higher, Papa!" she heard Thomas demand, his cheeks red with cold and excitement as he tried to place a lump of coal for the snowman's eye. "Make him tall like you!"

Edmund laughed, the sound carrying clearly through the still air, and lifted the boy onto his shoulders so he could reach the snowman's head. "There you go, my lad. But mind you don't fall—your mama will have my head if I bring you in covered in snow and sniffles on Christmas Eve."

Watching them together, Opal felt her heart swell with the same wonder that had filled her every day for the past five years. The life they had built in this peaceful corner of York-shire was everything she had dreamed of during those dark years at Ashford Manor, but more precious because it had been earned through sacrifice and struggle rather than simply granted by fortune.

The cottage itself was modest but comfortable, with low-beamed ceilings, wide fireplaces, and windows that looked out over rolling fields and distant hills. Edmund had purchased it, choosing this remote location not just for its beauty but for the anonymity it offered. Here, they were simply Mr. and Mrs. Ashford—he known as a gentleman farmer who had come north for his health, she as his devoted wife who ran the village school with remarkable skill for someone so young.

It had taken time for the villagers to warm to them, particularly when whispered rumours reached Millbrook about their dramatic past. But gradually, through simple acts of kindness and Edmund's willingness to work alongside his neighbors during harvest time, they had earned acceptance and eventually genuine affection from their community.

The transformation in Edmund never ceased to amaze her. Gone was the privileged young lord who had once worried about the proper forms of address for servants. In his place stood a man whose hands bore honest calluses from farm work, whose clothes were practical rather than fashionable, and whose greatest joy came from teaching his son to tend their small vegetable garden. The title and wealth he had inherited meant nothing to him now—indeed, he had formally renounced his claim to the Ashford name and fortune, which had been seized by the Crown and distributed among his father's victims' families.

"Mama, look!" Thomas's voice carried through the window as he proudly displayed the completed snowman. "We made him just like Grandpapa Samuel!"

Opal's throat tightened with emotion at the words. They had told Thomas stories about her father from the moment he was old enough to understand, ensuring that Samuel Hartwell's memory lived on in the next generation. To their son, Grandpapa Samuel was a hero who had fought for truth and justice, a brave man who had never given up hope even in his darkest hours.

The cottage door opened with a gust of cold air as Edmund and Thomas tumbled inside, both laughing and covered with snow despite Edmund's earlier cautions.

"Opal, you should see our masterpiece," Edmund called, hanging his coat on the peg by the door. "Thomas has inherited your artistic eye—the snowman looks remarkably dignified despite having a carrot for a nose."

"And buttons made from coal!" Thomas added importantly, racing to Opal's side and wrapping his small arms around her waist. "Is Great-grandmama's Christmas pudding ready?"

"Speaking of which," Opal said, ruffling her son's dark hair, "the pudding is nearly ready, and our guests will arrive soon. Why don't you help Papa set the table while I check on the goose?"

Their Christmas Eve tradition had evolved over the years into something that would have seemed impossible during Opal's time as a servant. Tonight, they would welcome a gathering that represented every stage of their journey—from the darkest moments of struggle to the brightest celebrations of triumph.

Thomas Whitmore would arrive first, as he always did, bearing gifts for young Thomas and the latest news from his inn, which had become a regular stop for travellers who wanted to hear the true story of Lord Ashford's downfall. The innkeeper had become like a beloved uncle to their small family, his gruff exterior hiding a heart that delighted in children's laughter and found deep satisfaction in their happiness.

Sir Richard Thornfield would come with his wife, bringing the perspective of London's legal community and updates on the ongoing reforms that had followed in the wake of Lord Ashford's trial. The corruption investigation had ultimately reached into the highest levels of government, resulting in dozens of dismissals and prosecutions that had helped restore public faith in the justice system.

But perhaps most remarkably, they expected Margaret and Henry Fletcher—the daughter and son-in-law of Tobias Fletcher, the merchant whose murder had started this entire chain of events. The Fletchers had sought out Opal and Edmund two years before, not for vengeance but for understanding, wanting to know how their father's death had finally led to justice. What began as a difficult conversation had blossomed into genuine friendship, with the Fletchers becoming regular visitors who found comfort in knowing that Tobias's death had not been meaningless.

"Mama," Thomas said as he carefully placed forks beside each plate on their dining table, "will you tell the Christmas story tonight? About baby Jesus and the star?"

"Of course, my darling," Opal replied, stirring the goose's rich gravy with one hand while adjusting the holly wreaths with the other. "But you must remember that Christmas is about more than just the story—it's about hope coming into a dark world, about love being stronger than fear."

"Like when Papa chose you instead of being rich?" Thomas asked with the startling directness that only children possessed.

Edmund paused in his arrangement of the candlesticks, meeting Opal's eyes across the table with a smile that held five years of shared memories. "Exactly like that, son. Sometimes the most important choices we make seem impossible at the time, but they turn out to be the ones that bring us the greatest happiness."

As if summoned by their conversation, the sound of carriage wheels on the lane announced the arrival of their first guests. Thomas raced to the window, his face pressed against the glass as he watched Thomas Whitmore's familiar figure emerge from a hired coach.

"Uncle Thomas is here!" the boy announced, using the honorary title they had bestowed on the innkeeper. "And he's carrying a big bag!"

Whitmore's entrance filled the cottage with good cheer and the crisp scent of winter air. Age had been kind to him—his hair was whiter now, his movements perhaps a bit slower, but his eyes still held the same shrewd intelligence that had made him such a valuable ally during their darkest hours.

"Young Master Thomas," he said formally, bowing low to the delighted child. "I trust you've been good this year? Father Christmas has been making inquiries, you know."

"I've been very good," Thomas assured him seriously. "I helped Papa with the harvest, and I learned my letters, and I only pulled the cat's tail twice."

"Only twice?" Whitmore raised an eyebrow in mock surprise. "Why, that's practically saintly behaviour. I believe Father Christmas will be most impressed."

As Whitmore distributed his gifts—a wooden horse for Thomas, books for Edmund and Opal, and a bottle of his finest brandy for the evening's festivities—more guests arrived in quick succession. The cottage filled with conversation and laughter as friends settled around the warmth of the fire, sharing the latest news from their various corners of the world.

Sir Richard brought word that the legal reforms inspired by Lord Ashford's case were spreading throughout the empire, with colonial administrators being held to new standards of accountability. Margaret Fletcher shared updates from her father's old trading partners, many of whom had contributed to a memorial fund that helped other victims of violence along England's roads.

But it was Henry Fletcher who provided the evening's most significant news, pulling Edmund aside during the pre-dinner conversation with an expression of barely contained excitement.

"I've had word from London," he said quietly, glancing around to ensure he wouldn't be overheard. "The Home Secretary wants to meet with you and Opal in the new year. There's talk of establishing a new investigative body—something that would prevent cases like Lord Ashford's from being covered up in the future."

Edmund's eyes widened with interest. "What sort of investigative body?"

"One that reports directly to Parliament rather than local magistrates," Henry explained. "Officials who can't be bought or intimidated by regional power brokers. They want to use your case as the foundation for something that could protect ordinary citizens throughout the kingdom."

The implications were staggering. After years of quiet contentment in their rural retreat, they were being offered the chance to help shape the very system of justice that had nearly failed them so catastrophically.

"What do you think?" Edmund asked, seeking Opal's opinion as he always did on matters of importance.

"I think," Opal said slowly, one hand moving instinctively to her growing belly, "that my father would say we have a responsibility to help others avoid the suffering we endured. But I also think we need to consider what's best for our family."

Before Edmund could respond, young Thomas appeared at his side, tugging urgently on his father's sleeve. "Papa, Uncle Thomas says it's time for dinner, and I'm so hungry I could eat the whole goose!"

The conversation about London would have to wait. Tonight was Christmas Eve, a time for celebration and gratitude rather than weighty decisions about the future. As they gathered around their modest dining table, with candlelight flickering across the faces of friends who had become family, Opal felt the same sense of completion that had sustained her through five years of happiness.

The goose was perfectly roasted, the pudding rich with fruit and brandy, the conversation flowing as freely as the wine Edmund had carefully selected from his small but cherished cellar. Thomas regaled their guests with an elaborate story about the snowman's adventures, while Whitmore shared gossip from the inn that had everyone laughing until their sides ached.

But it was when they gathered around the fire for the evening's traditional storytelling that the true spirit of their Christmas celebration emerged. Opal settled into her favorite chair with Thomas on her lap, Edmund beside her with his hand resting on her shoulder, their friends arranged in a comfortable circle that seemed to embody everything good about human fellowship.

"Tell us about Grandpapa Samuel," Thomas requested, as he did every Christmas Eve. "Tell us about how he was brave and good and never gave up."

Opal's voice was soft but clear as she began the story their son knew by heart but never tired of hearing—how Samuel Hartwell had witnessed a great wrong and refused to remain silent, how he had sacrificed everything to gather evidence of the truth, how his courage had ultimately led to justice for many innocent people.

"But the most important thing about Grandpapa Samuel," she concluded, "wasn't that he was brave, although he was. It wasn't that he was good, although he was that too. The most important thing was that he never stopped believing that love was stronger than hate, that truth was more powerful than lies, and that ordinary people could change the world if they had the courage to try."

"Like you and Papa did," Thomas said with satisfaction. "You changed the world, too."

"We helped," Edmund corrected gently. "But the real heroes were people like Uncle Thomas, who risked their own safety to help strangers. People like Sir Richard, who chose justice over convenience. People like the Fletchers, who chose forgiveness over revenge. Change happens when many people make small choices to do what's right."

As the evening progressed and their guests took their leave, promising to return for Boxing Day festivities, Opal found herself standing once again at the kitchen window, watching snow fall softly over their peaceful village. Edmund came up behind her, his arms encircling her waist, his chin resting on her shoulder as they looked out together at the winter night.

"Happy?" he asked, though he already knew the answer.

"Perfectly," Opal replied, leaning back against his warmth. "Sometimes I can hardly believe this is our life now. After everything we went through, to end up here, with Thomas, with another baby coming, with friends who feel like family..."

"It doesn't seem real sometimes," Edmund agreed. "But then I remember that we earned this happiness. Every moment of it was paid for with courage and sacrifice and the refusal to accept that things had to remain the way they were."

They stood in comfortable silence for several minutes, watching the snow transform their garden into a winter wonderland. Somewhere in the distance, church bells began to chime midnight, calling the faithful to Christmas services across the countryside.

"And someday, Opal, someday my mother's heart will open, and she will join us in our Christmas celebration."

Opal's eyes misted over. This sentiment was spoken every year by her dear husband, and she sincerely prayed it would someday come true.

"Now, we should decide about London," Edmund said eventually. "About the Home Secretary's proposal."

Opal was quiet for a long moment, considering all the implications of returning to public life, of once again placing their family in the spotlight of national attention. The cottage in Millbrook represented safety, privacy, the chance to raise their children away from the scrutiny that had once threatened to destroy them.

But it also represented a retreat from the larger world, a turning away from the very mission that had brought them together in the first place.

"Do you remember what you said to me that first night we met at the mill?" she asked finally. "About how your father's crimes were bigger than just one family's tragedy?"

"I remember," Edmund said softly.

"Well, corruption and injustice are bigger than just Lord Ashford's crimes," Opal continued. "If we have the chance to help prevent other families from suffering what we suffered, don't we have an obligation to try?"

Edmund's arms tightened around her. "Even if it means leaving all this? Even if it means raising our children in London, surrounded by the very people who once wanted to destroy us?"

"Even then," Opal said firmly. "My father didn't sacrifice everything so that we could live quietly in the countryside. He did it so that justice would prevail, so that ordinary people would have someone to turn to when the powerful tried to crush them."

"Then we'll go," Edmund decided. "We'll accept the Home Secretary's proposal and see if we can help build something that will outlast both of us. Something that will ensure Thomas and his sibling grow up in a world where truth and justice aren't luxuries that only the wealthy can afford."

As they prepared for bed that Christmas Eve, moving through the familiar rituals of banking the fire and checking on their sleeping son, Opal felt the same sense of anticipation that had sustained her through the darkest moments of their struggle. The future was uncertain, filled with new challenges and unknown dangers, but it was also bright with possibility.

In the morning, they would wake to Christmas Day in their perfect cottage, surrounded by the peace and contentment they had worked so hard to achieve. They would exchange gifts, share another wonderful meal with their friends, and watch Thomas's face light up with wonder at the magic of the season.

But after the holidays, they would begin preparing for a new chapter in their lives—one that would take them back to the world of politics and power, back to the fight for justice that had defined their courtship and early marriage. It would not be easy, and there would undoubtedly be those who resented their return to prominence.

But they would face it together, as they had faced everything else, sustained by a love that had been tested in the fires of adversity and proven stronger than any force arrayed against it.

As Opal settled into bed beside the man who had chosen her, she touched the small wooden cross that still hung around her neck—the gift from a stranger whose brother had been one of Lord Ashford's victims. She had worn it every day for five years, a reminder that their victory had been won not just for themselves but for all those whose voices had been silenced by corruption and greed.

Tomorrow would bring Christmas joy and family celebration. Next year would bring new challenges and fresh opportunities to serve the cause of justice. But tonight, on this holy eve when Christians celebrated the birth of hope into a dark world, Opal Ashford was content to simply lie beside her husband and listen to the soft breathing of their son in the next room.

The blacksmith's daughter had found her happy ending. But more than that, she had found her purpose—to ensure that other daughters, other families, other ordinary people who stood up against injustice would not have to face their battles alone.

The snow continued to fall outside their cottage windows, blanketing the world in pristine white that seemed to promise fresh starts and new beginnings. And in the warm sanctuary of their home, surrounded by love and sustained by hope, Opal drifted off to sleep with a prayer of gratitude for all they had been given and a promise to use those gifts in service of something greater than themselves.

Christmas had come to Millbrook village, bringing with it all the ancient promises of peace and goodwill, of love triumphant over hate, of light shining in the darkness. And in one small cottage where a former servant slept beside a noble-man's son, where their child dreamed of snowmen and Christmas pudding, those promises felt as real and tangible as the gentle snow that continued to fall through the holy night.

The End

CONTINUE READING...

THANK you for reading ***Christmas Secrets at Ashford Manor!* Are you wondering what to read next?** Why not read ***The Orphan's Savior?* Here's a sneak peek for you:**

June 11th, 1860

The warm wind blew around her on this fine summer's day. An inquisitive squirrel scurried toward her, stopped, and stared straight at her. Its large, black eyes didn't blink. Then it turned to its left and scurried toward a tree, climbing it as if its life depended on it. Ten-year-old Ava March watched it without feeling, a sense of acceptance and calm before her as she sat next to the unmarked grave of her dear mam. She'd miss her, she would.

Ava cursed the heavens for taking her mother away from her. She was all she had; there was no one else. She didn't even have a father, whom she was told had fled as soon as she was born. Ava never knew him, and so she didn't miss having a father. Her mother was the one who cared for her, who raised her through many difficulties.

A bluebird chirped on a low branch, bringing Ava back to the present. But it was hard because bits of memory of playing with her mother came to her. Like the days when they threw snowballs at each other in the wintertime and laughed till their stomachs hurt. Then there were days when they would jump into the river on hot, scorching afternoons and swim through the cool water. Ava could not remember a time when they didn't have fun, when they didn't enjoy each other's company.

Absently, she scratched her knee where the coarse wool of her dress irritated her skin. She looked down at the earthy mound of her mother's grave and placed a single daisy there.

"I'll miss you, Mam," she whispered. "I'll never forget ya."

Ava stood up, feeling thirsty, the sun hot on her head. Fatigued, she walked away and onto a short road, where carriages, horse-carts, and bullock carts passed. She thought of place in the river where she could drink. It wasn't far from here, for which she was grateful. A black cat crossed her path, and Ava gave a start. She was superstition, and black cats were bad luck.

But what else could go wrong now? She had already lost her mother. Then, it dawned on her that she truly was all alone, and she was only ten. But she wasn't afraid of what lay ahead of her. She knew she could get on, and she would do it. She had watched and helped her mother wash clothes, cook food on the hearth, and even sew. Her mother taught her all these skills from the age of five.

"One day, you will need to do all this, sweet Ava," her mother's beautiful voice had told her one winter's day, which had been one of the hardest times she could remember.

This year's winter was harsh too, and it seemed to always be snowing fast and hard. The ground was covered in no time, which was a delight for her for a time, but not when the fire went out, and the house was filled with freezing air. At last, she came to a cleaner section of the river and knelt over the edge, dipping her small hand in the cool water and putting a palmful into her mouth. It was very satisfying, and it made her feel so much better. She had her fill and walked the rest of the way home.

Click Here to Continue Reading!

https://www.ticahousepublishing.com/victorian-romance.html

THANKS FOR READING

If you love **Victorian Romance**, <u>**Click Here**</u>

https://victorian.subscribemenow.com/

to hear about all <u>**New Faye Godwin Romance Releases!**</u> **I will let you know as soon as they become available!**

Thank you, Friends! If you enjoyed *Christmas Secrets at Ashford Manor,* would you kindly take a couple minutes to leave a positive review on Amazon? It only takes a moment, and positive reviews truly make a difference. Thank you so much! I appreciate it!

Much love,

Faye Godwin

MORE FAYE GODWIN VICTORIAN ROMANCES!

We love rich, dramatic Victorian Romances and have a library of Faye Godwin titles just for you! (Remember that ALL of Faye's Victorian titles can be downloaded FREE with Kindle Unlimited!)

CLICK HERE to discover Faye's Complete Collection of Victorian Romance!

https://ticahousepublishing.com/victorian-romance.html

ABOUT THE AUTHOR

Faye Godwin has been fascinated with Victorian Romance since she was a teen. After reading every Victorian Romance in her public library, she decided to start writing them herself —which she's been doing ever since. Faye lives with her husband and young son in England. She loves to travel throughout her country, dreaming up new plots for her romances. She's delighted to join the Tica House Publishing family and looks forward to getting to know her readers.

contact@ticahousepublishing.com

Printed in Dunstable, United Kingdom